P9-CEY-448

LIFE: DNA SEQUENCE 160-61 ATG GTA TCC CGT AAG CAT GTG GCT CTG CTG GTG GTG CTG GCC TCC CAG ACG GAA GCC TTC GTC CCC ATG CTG AAG GAA CCC CGT GCS ACT GGG CTA CTG AAC GAA TTC GTA ATC CGG TCT AGG CCT GCG TCC GAA TCC CTG GAA GAT GGA TCT TTT TGC AAG GAA GTC GTA GTT CCG GTC TAC TCG TCA GGA TAG AGG TCT TTT CGT GAA AAG CTG ATG TTG GCC CTG CAT GCT ACT AGG GAT GAT GGA TCT TTT

HOLY EVOLUTION!" GASPS FRANK EINSTEIN, CROUCHED BEHIND a log. "Talk about All Interconnected Life. This is amazing."

Two towering figures step forward.

"This is such great proof. From microscopic bugs . . . to the biggest beasts. We all evolved. We are *all* connected."

Up in the tree, Watson nods. He is not thinking this is so amazing. He is thinking this is crazy. He is thinking this is scary.

He would say something. But he can't.

And he really would like to, because he is seriously worried that this time Frank Einstein will not be able to think his way out of a jam.

"Don't worry, Watson," says Frank. "I'll think of something."

"BBBAAWWWKKKKRRR!" growls the megapredator.

"CHHHHKKKKCHHHKKKKK!" rattles the monster next to it.

Both slowly turn and look at the humans crouched behind the log.

"Uh-oh" says Frank Einstein, suddenly realizing what it feels like to not be kings of the food chain. "It's survival of the *smartest* now."

FRA
EINS

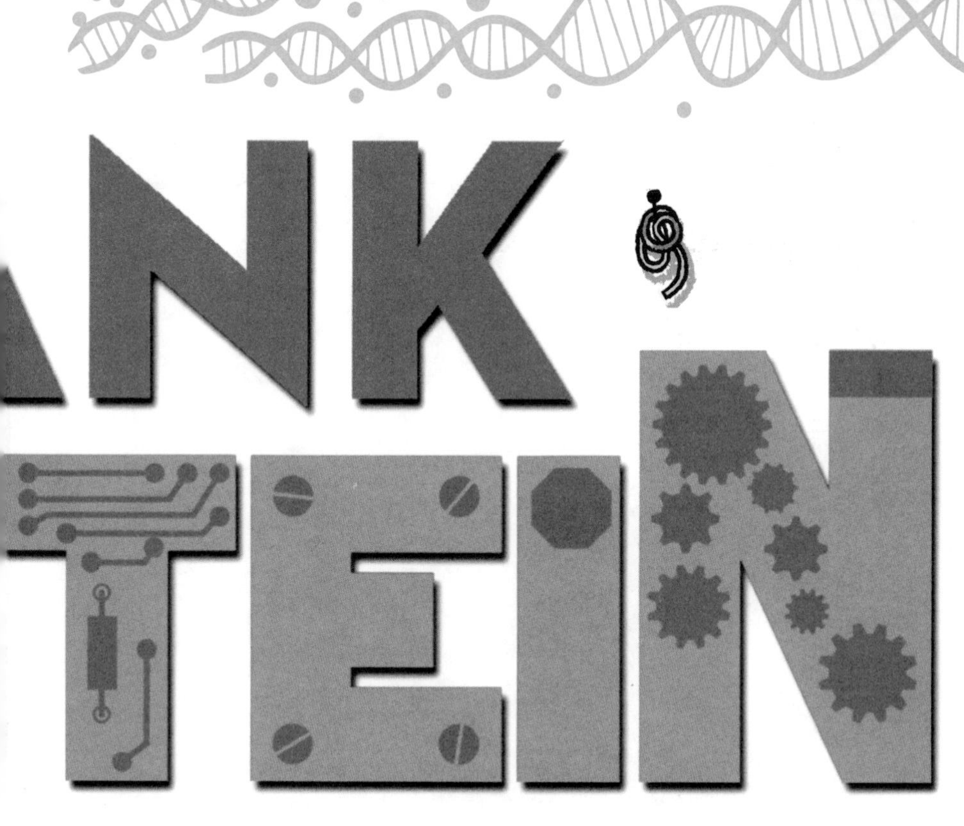

and the EVOBLASTER BELT

JON SCIESZKA

ILLUSTRATED BY BRIAN BIGGS

AMULET BOOKS
LONDON

A
B
C
D
E
F
G

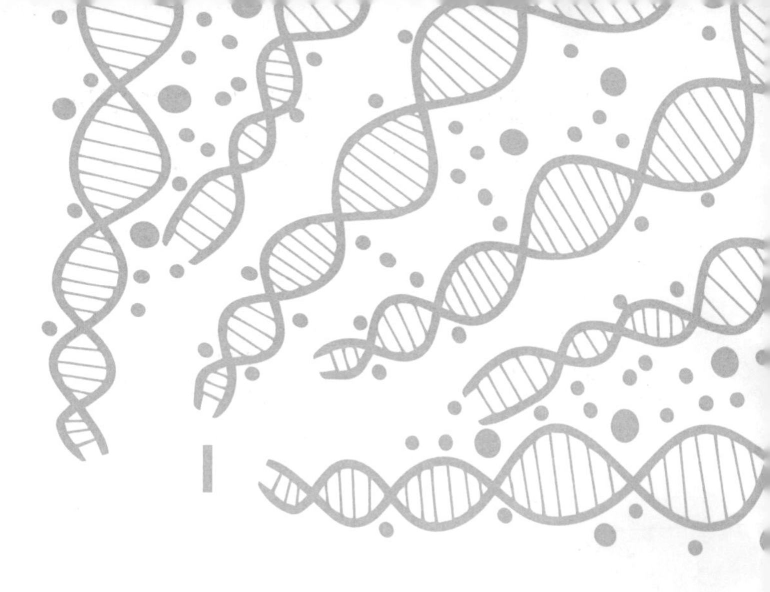

1

AN ORANGE-AND-BLACK AND WHITE-SPOTTED MONARCH BUTTERFLY **(A)** flaps its wings and . . .

. . . gets chomped in the jaws of a sticky-tongued green-and-black leopard frog **(B)** . . .

. . . that gets suddenly swallowed by a leaping largemouth bass **(C)** . . .

. . . that gets snagged by the sharp talons of a swooping red-tailed hawk **(D)** . . .

. . . that gets clawed by a jumping orange-and-white-striped house cat **(E)** . . .

. . . that gets chased through the woods by a barking hound dog **(F)** . . .

. . . that suddenly stops when it hears two humans yelling **(G)** . . .

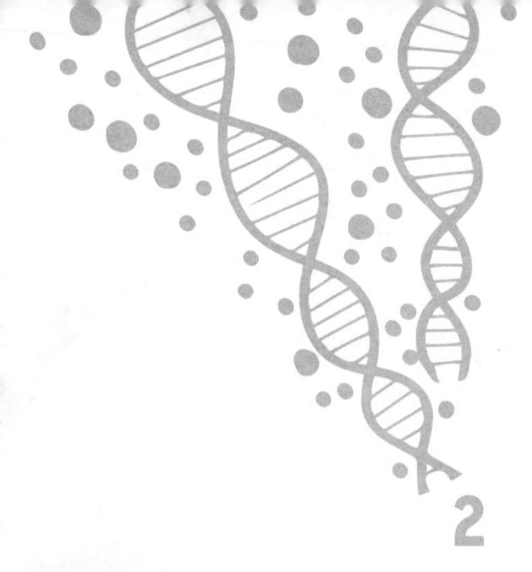

2

HEAD BUTT!"

"Spin Kick!"

The hound dog stares at the two small humans battling each other in the meadow.

"Bear Hug!"

"Airplane Spin!"

The dog doesn't smell any food. It wonders what the humans are fighting over.

"Butt Drop!"

"Leg Lock!"

A bigger human appears at the edge of the clearing.

"Frank! Watson!" calls Grampa Al. "How about a little help putting up the tents?"

"Awww," says Frank Einstein.

"I totally had you pinned," says his pal Watson.

Frank releases Watson from his headlock. Watson releases Frank from his leg lock.

"And let's show some hustle!" calls Grampa Al. "Because Atomic Al wouldn't want to have to take you down with his Nuclear Piledriver." He bends forward, flexing his arms into a wrestling pose.

Watson looks at Frank in surprise. "Did he just say 'Atomic Al'? Does that mean your Grampa Al used to wrestle?"

Frank brushes the dirt and grass off his pants. "I never asked. But I would not be surprised."

The hound dog snorts and trots off into the woods.

The orange-and-white-striped house cat, sitting safely high in a maple tree, licks its right paw.

Frank gives Watson his hand and helps him up. Watson picks his flashy gold championship-wrestling belt off a nearby bush and flips it over one shoulder. "This championship match will be continued later," says Watson.

Frank grabs the belt. "You were two seconds away from tapping out." He raises the belt overhead. "Wooooooorld Chaaaaampion—FFFFFrrrrraaaaaank EINSTEIN!"

Watson karate chops Frank and takes back the belt. "No way! I had you right where I wanted you."

The two guys laugh. They stop, stand in the middle of the meadow, and take in the sight of the sunlit clouds in a deep-blue sky overhead, the sound of a bee buzzing circles around the flowering clover, the smell of the pond behind them, and the trees all around them.

"How great is this?" says Watson. "Deep woods. Pure vacation. Nothing to do but goof around and relax."

Frank looks at the bee, the flower, the hawk overhead, the cat perched up in the tree. He sees something different. "It's relaxing for us. Because we are the top of the food chain. But look around, Watson. We forget that we are part of all this. Everything living is connected.

"And it's kind of perfect this is Darwin State Park. Because it was scientist Charles Darwin who called life the Struggle for Existence. Every minute of every day—eat or be eaten."

"OK, that's depressing," says Watson. "But at least we get a vacation from that sneaky T. Edison and his evil Mr. Chimp. And we get to go fishing."

Frank whacks Watson's championship belt. "Because we are *kings of the food chain.*"

"And it's good to be the king."

"And it's good to relax for a change, and not have to fix emergencies . . ."

The guys walk through the meadow and hop the stream toward the tents.

A bang, splintering wood, a yell, a crash, the *whoooop whoop whoop* of a siren split the sunset calm of the woods.

"Spoke too soon," says Frank.

He and Watson run for the tents.

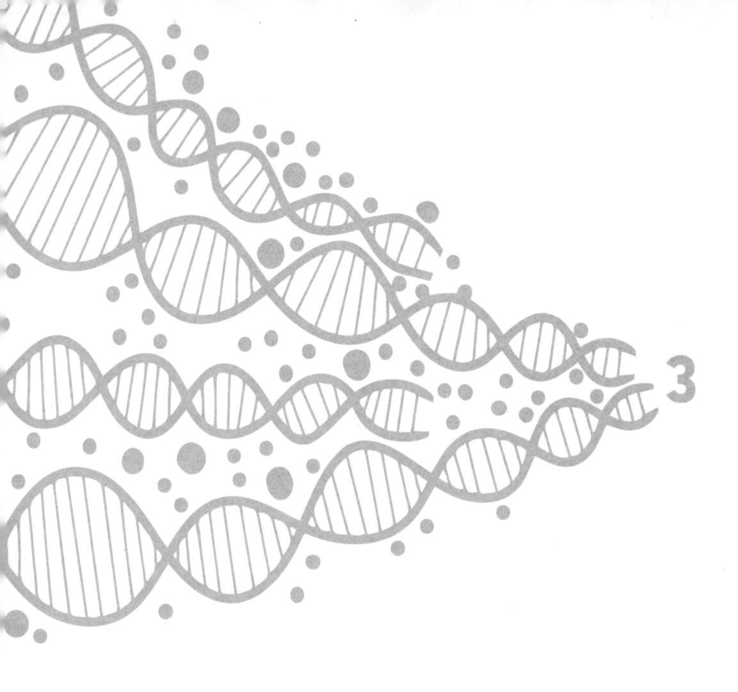

WEEEEEE-OOOOOO, WEEEEEE-OOOOOO, WEEEEEE-OOOOOOOOO!" wails something in the middle of the Darwin State Park woods.

"Yaah! Hooo! Haaah!" Wild yells add to the din.

A startled flock of crows explodes into the sky, flapping and cawing.

Frightened squirrels, rabbits, and field mice run, hop, scramble for safety.

Frank and Watson stop at the edge of the campsite and see where all the noise and commotion is coming from—a gigantic pile of dead tree branches jumping and shaking and howling.

Right where their tents used to be.

"WEEEEEE-OOOOOOOO, WEEEEEE-OOOOOOOO, WEEEEEE-OOOOOOOO!"

"Yaah! Hooo! Haaah!"

"Oh man," says Watson. "Maybe we are not the kings of the food chain after all. Something *huge* is eating our tents!"

Frank picks up a hefty broken tree branch and swings it like a club. "And it's attacking Grampa Al! We have to save him! Come on!"

"Wait! What if it's Bigfoot?!"

"Then you can use your Head Butt."

Frank charges down the hill toward the thrashing, howling pile of craziness.

"Look big!" yells Frank. "And noisy! And mean!"

"WEEEEEE-OOOOOOOO, WEEEEEE-OOOOOOOO, WEEEEEE-OOOOOOOO!"

"Yaah! Hooo! Haaah!"

Frank and Watson jump on the pile of branches.

"We'll save you, Grampa!" yells Frank.

He smashes the branches covering the tents. "Take that!"

Watson head butts whatever it is under the tent fabric.

"Owwwwwwww."

"WEEEEEE-OOOOOOOO, WEEEEEE-OOOOOOOO, WEEEEEE-OOOOOOOO!"

"Yaah! Hooo! Haaah!"

Something grabs Frank, wrapping him in a crushing python grip.

Frank kicks and struggles, but he can't move.

Watson rolls on the ground, holding his aching head.

"WEEEEEE-OOOOOOOO, WEEEEEE-OOOOOOOO, WEEEEEE-OOOOOOOO!"

"Yaah! Hooo! Haaah!"

The mess of branches, leaves, and wiggling tent suddenly blows apart.

And Frank and Watson see the monster that has been making all the noise.

"WEEEEEE–OOOOOO, WEEEEEE . . . oh . . . ," screeches a small robot.

"Klink!" says Frank.

"Yaah! Hooo . . . oops," says Grampa Al, still punching and kicking, with his glasses knocked sideways.

"Fighting with Grampa Al?" says Watson.

Frank turns to look at the Bigfoot holding him. But it is not Bigfoot. "Klank? What are you guys doing?"

"Grampa Al told me to get a lot of wood," answers Klank.

Grampa Al adjusts his glasses. "I probably should have been more specific about not delivering *a whole tree*. I thought we were under attack. I went into defense mode. And then Klink started freaking out."

Klink straightens his webcam. "I was not '*freaking out*.' The force of the falling plant life activated my new security alarm."

Klank lowers Frank to the ground.

"Darn," says Watson. "I thought we had found Bigfoot."

Grampa Al looks up at the setting sun. He calculates that they have about another half hour of good daylight. "We've got something bigger than Bigfoot. We've got a mission that has come from the Very Top."

"Ohhh, nice!" says Watson, pulling out his magnifying glass. "A secret spy mission? What is it? What is it?"

Grampa Al pulls the collapsed tent out of the pile of

branches. "Let's get our tents up first. Then I'll answer all your questions."

"Oooo! Oooo!" beeps Klank. **"I have a question. How can you tell if an elephant has been in your refrigerator?"**

Klink spins his head around in an annoyed twirl. "*What?* This better not be one of your illogical jokes."

"Hmmmmmmm?" buzzes Klank.

"Because I do not want to hear something that does not make sense. That makes me burn out my brain circuits."

Watson laughs. "Well, I'd like to know. How *can* you tell if an elephant has been in your refrigerator?"

"If you see elephant footprints in the butter."

Watson cracks up laughing.

"Ha. Ha. Ha."

"Bzzzzzzzrrrrrrr," says Klink. "No! That cannot be true. Bzzzzzzz." Klink's brain circuits try to make sense of an elephant in a refrigerator. Klink's brain circuits start to overheat.

Watson laughs harder.

"Ha. Ha. Ha."

"Elephant . . . refrigerator . . . footprints . . . noooooooooooo!"

Phooomp!

Klink blows a brain circuit and shuts down.

"Aw shoot," says Frank. "I wish you guys wouldn't do that. Now we have to reboot Klink. Again."

Grampa Al claps his hands. "OK! Let's get cracking! Tents up. Then I'll tell you what we are really doing here."

Crickets begin to chirp.

An owl hoots.

"Because we are not here just for the camping . . ."

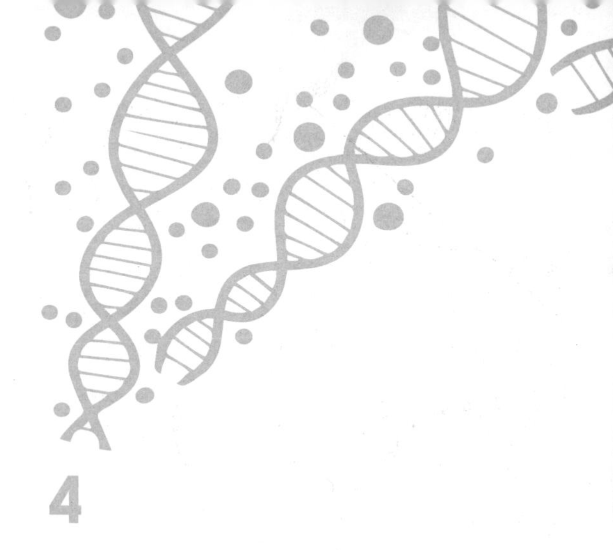

4

FRANK, WATSON, KLINK, KLANK, AND GRAMPA AL SIT AROUND A small fire inside a circle of stones just outside their tent.

Bluish-white stars dot the inky night sky.

One unseen cricket chirps in the dark beyond the firelight.

Frank checks his watch and counts the number of chirps in fourteen seconds. He adds forty and calculates, "Seventy-two degrees."

"How do you know that?" asks Watson.

Klink beeps. "The number of cricket chirps in fourteen seconds plus forty gives a fairly accurate estimate of the atmosphere's temperature in degrees Fahrenheit."

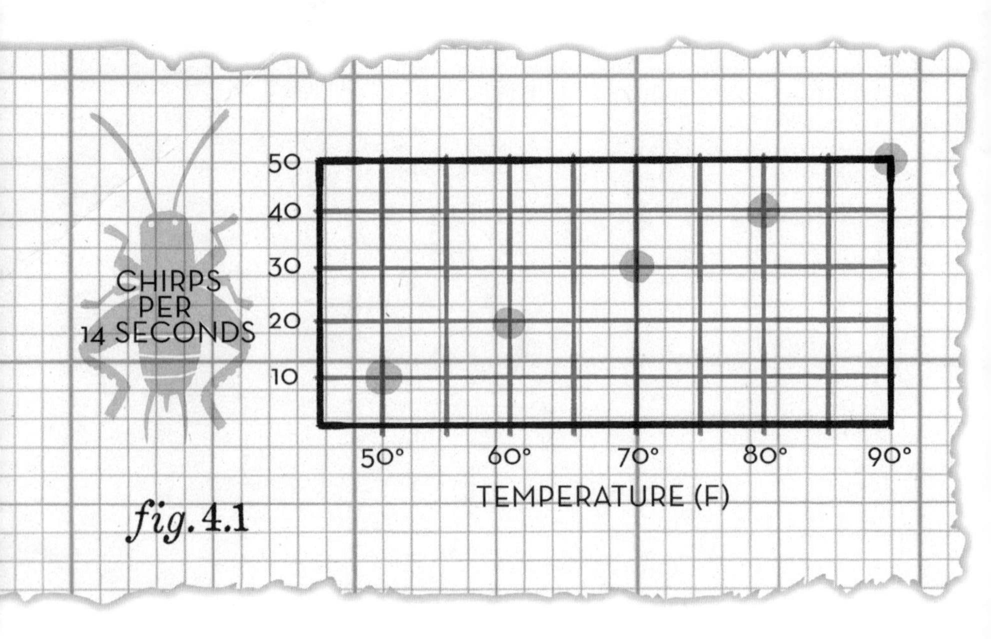

fig. 4.1

"Seriously? Wow," says Watson. He turns to Grampa Al. "But let's hear more about our secret spy mission."

"Yeah!" says Frank, holding his hot dog roasting stick over the red-orange heat of the fire. "You should have told us when we were packing. I would have brought some of the inventions I've been working on. Like my Night-Vision Specs. My Super Silencer. My Complete Camouflage Cloak."

"And I would have brought my Spy Sneakers," says Watson.

Grampa Al spins his hot dog over the fire.

"Sorry I didn't tell you sooner. But I couldn't risk a leak."

Grampa Al puts his perfectly roasted hot dog in a perfectly toasted bun.

"And let's just say this is a camping trip . . . with a little extra research. Which is what I told your mom and dad so they wouldn't worry about us. And why we brought along Klink for background intel . . ."

"Very smart of you," says Klink. "Because I have seriously enhanced my attachments for outdoor research." Klink pops out a microscope, a magnifying glass, a telescope, a hatchet, and a custom Three-Pronged Hot Dog Roasting Fork.

Grampa Al nods. "Nice. And Klank for muscle."

"Ooooo, oooo," says Klank. **"What is this button for?"** He pushes a green button on Klink's side.

"Do not press tha—" says Klink, too late.

A fishing pole, an umbrella, and a tiki torch all pop out of Klink—and he falls over on his side.

"Oops. Sorry," says Klank. He picks up Klink, folds in his new attachments, and sets him back on his feet. **"Are we still going to tell ghost stories?"**

Klink buzzes. "Klank, you are such a . . . grrrrrrrrr. *And* there is no scientific evidence for ghosts. So there is no need to tell stories about them."

"But I love spooky stories. And hot dogs!"

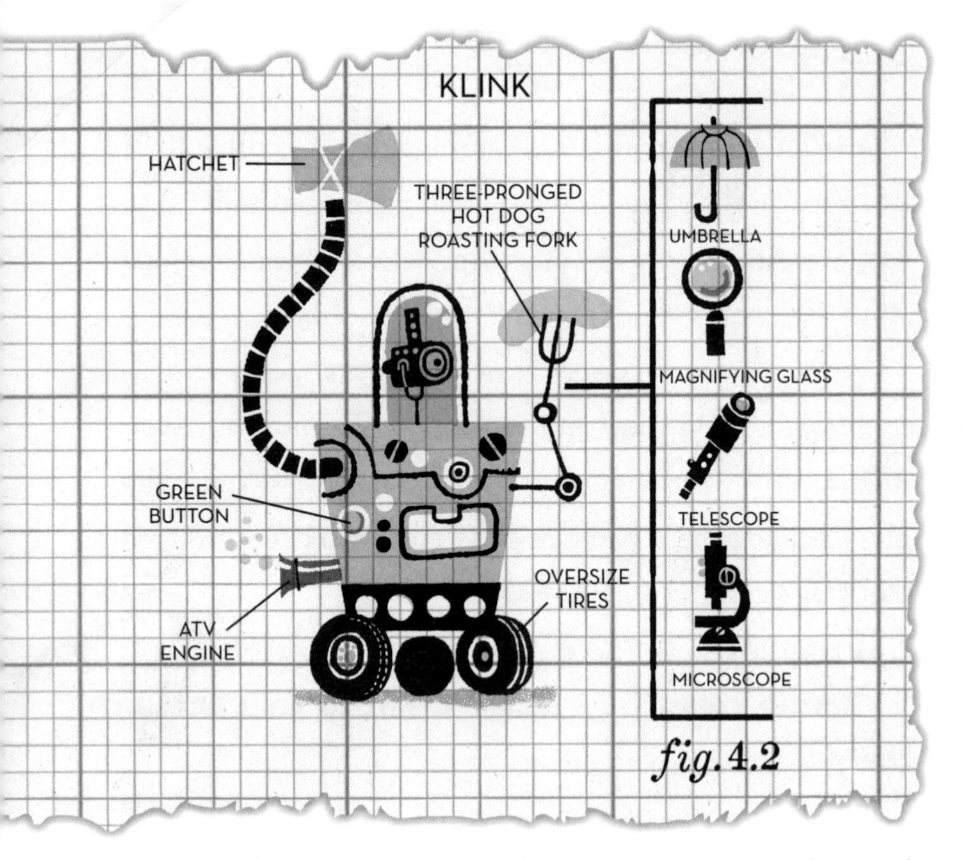

Frank finishes the last of his hot dog and leans forward. The firelight flickers shadows on his face. "We can tell spooky stories later. What is this mission?"

Grampa Al looks left and right into the dark woods surrounding their little circle of firelight. He lowers his voice. "Strange things have been happening out here in Darwin Park. Bees are dying. Frogs are disappearing. An entire cave of bats—gone. Something is seriously disrupting the life cycles up here."

Frank nods. "You mess with one part, you mess up everything."

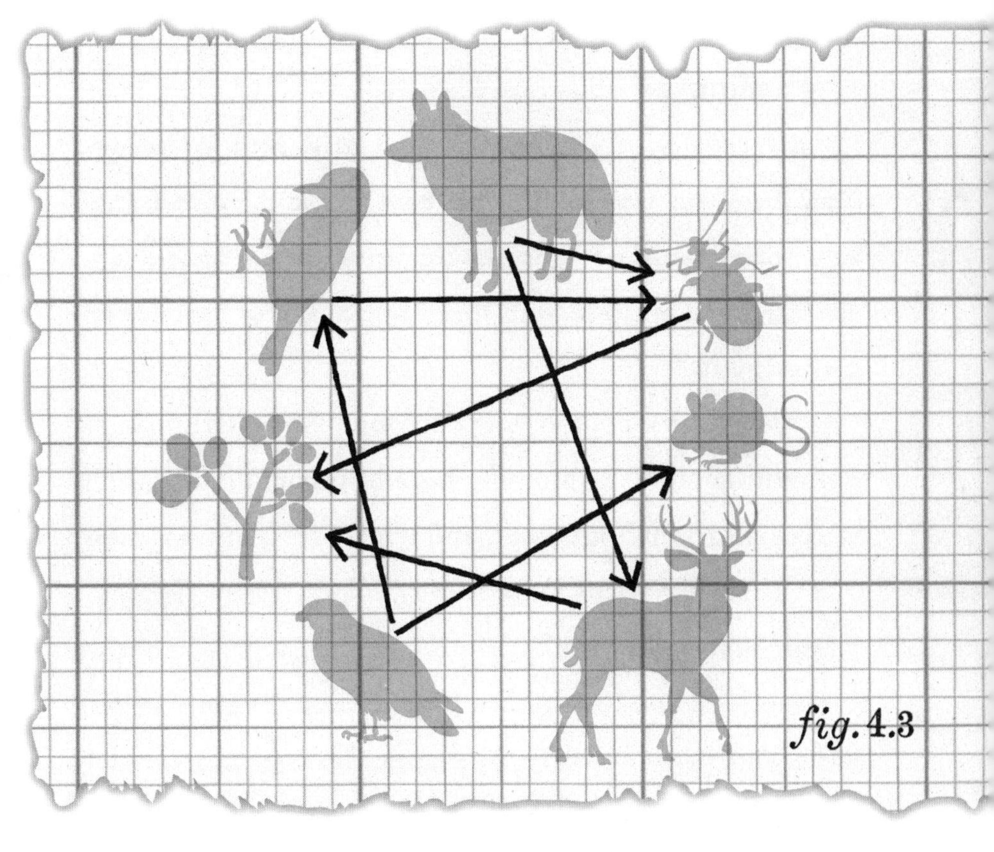

Grampa Al turns to Frank. "Exactly. And here's the mystery we are here to solve—any research teams that have been sent to this area, they have mysteriously lost all of their electronic data. And hikers and campers have reported being chased off by scary accidents . . . and strange animals. We need to find out what is happening."

"Bigfoot!" says Watson. "Or chupacabras! I knew it!"

"Or ghosts!" adds Klank.

"No," says Klink. "That is just the plot of every *Scooby-Doo* cartoon. The bad guys pretend they are monsters or ghosts to frighten Scooby and Shaggy and anyone else from uncovering their criminal activity."

"This is no *Scooby-Doo* cartoon," says Grampa Al. "Something bad is happening here in Darwin Park. And it is up to us to find out what, and who . . . is behind it."

The cricket chirps more slowly.

"Why us?" asks Frank.

Grampa Al pokes the fire with a stick. "I am working with some people to save the planet," he says mysteriously. "And I thought this could be a great fit with your plan to study All Connected Life."

Frank loves this idea. "Genius, Einstein!"

Grampa Al laughs, and answers, "Precisely. Genius, Einstein."

"Oh no," says Watson. "We are not going to go do something dangerous in the woods right now, are we?"

Grampa Al looks up at the almost-full moon. "Too late for anything tonight. Let's turn in. Get a good night's sleep. We'll get our orders and roll out first thing zero nine hundred hours."

"Roger that!" says Frank Einstein.

"What?" asks Klank.

"That's military talk for nine o'clock in the morning. And OK."

Klank splits a log with his metal hand. **"OK. But I do have one more question."**

"Ask away," says Grampa Al.

"Why did the elephant wear red toenail polish?"

"Nooooooooooooooooo!" buzzes Klink. He pops out a toilet-plunger attachment and plops it over Klank's mouth speaker.

Frank and Watson laugh.

Grampa Al scatters the fire's coals inside the stones so they safely burn out.

Everyone crawls into their sleeping bags for the night.

Klink and Klank power down.

The moon rises higher.

The red coals of the fire slowly fade to black.

The cricket falls silent. Not because the temperature has fallen. But because it has been disturbed by the footstep of something not human. By the footstep of humans' closest living primate relative.

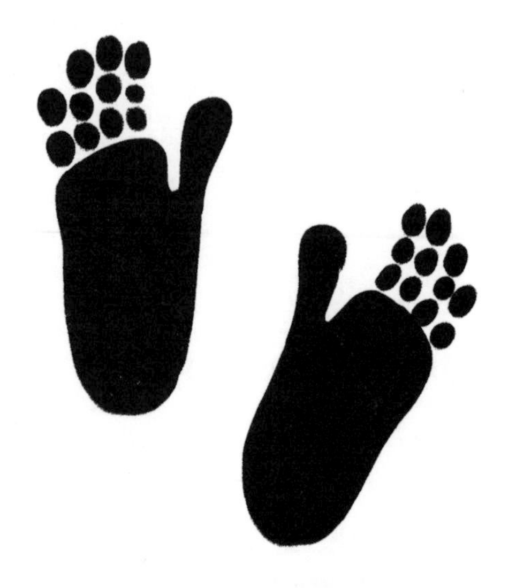

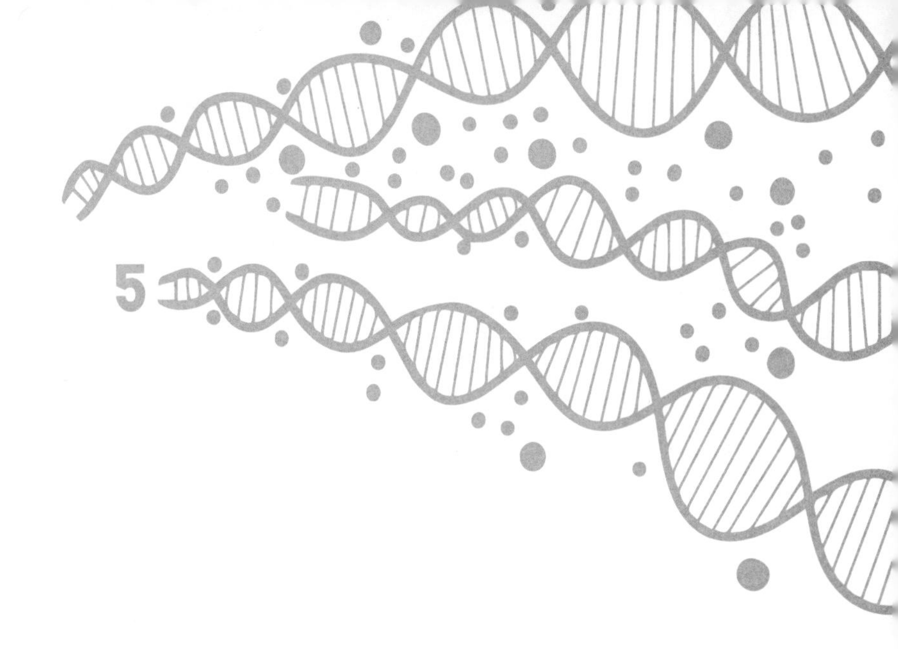

5

THE MORNING SUN RISES SLOWLY OVER A WOVEN BLACK METAL fence in the northern end of Darwin Park.

A kid with a bad haircut, green shorts, and size-five wing-tip shoes with black socks pulled up as high as they can go swings back and forth in a hammock tied between two trees. The kid is eating breakfast and looking at a blueprint of his new factory.

An orange-and-black butterfly flits across a neatly mowed lawn in front of the long, low black factory building that is built right on top of a rushing stream.

The kid is talking to a chimpanzee sitting in the lawn chair next to his hammock. The chimpanzee is wearing surf shorts, a Hawaiian shirt, and flip-flops. He is also

Nature Good

sipping a delicious frozen Banana ’n’ Ants breakfast drink of his own invention. This drink is decorated with one tiny pink umbrella.

“I have to say, Mr. Chimp,” begins T. Edison (because of course it is T. Edison. Who else wears wing tips with black socks and shorts?), “this is a genius idea.”

T. Edison takes a bite of banana muffin and a swig of water from a plastic bottle.

“Take something everyone gets for free. And sell it back to them as something fresh and brand-new. Genius!”

Mr. Chimp leans back in his lawn chair. He crosses his legs, takes a long slow sip of his Banana ’n’ Ants drink, and signs:

T. Edison swings in his hammock, happily watching the stream of water rushing into one end of the building, and coming out the other as a tiny trickle.

The orange-and-black butterfly flaps from flower to flower.

"Sometimes I amaze even myself with my genius ideas."

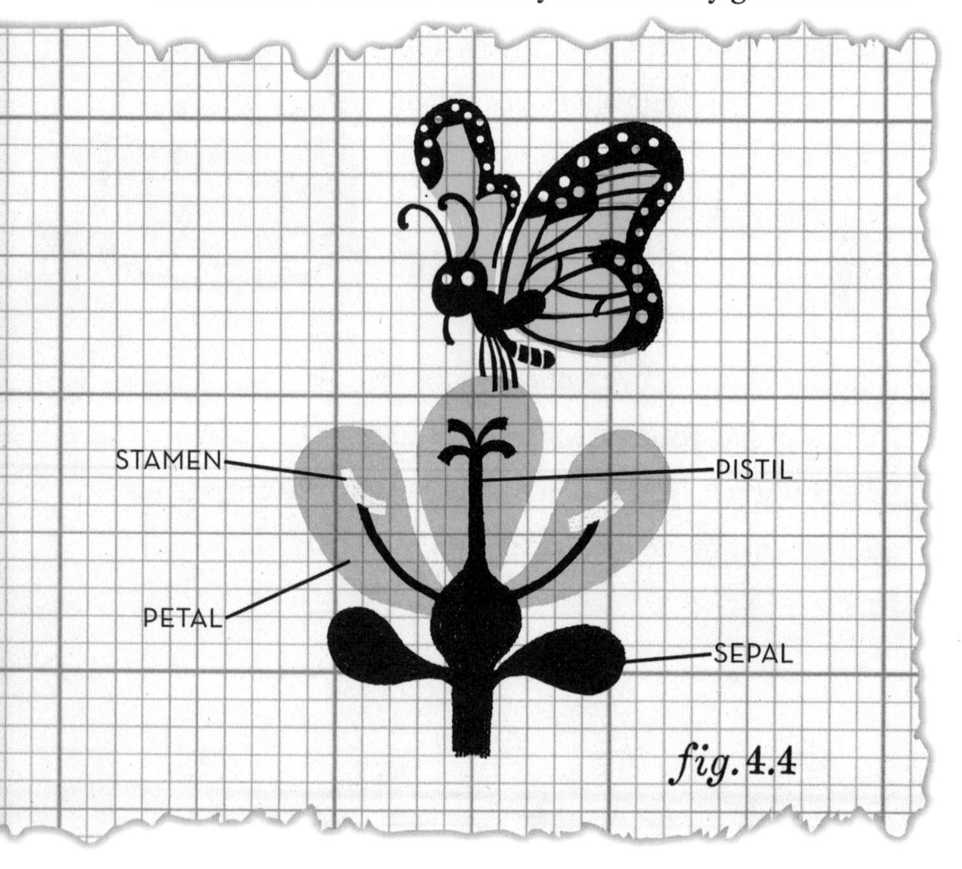

fig. 4.4

Mr. Chimp eyeballs T. Edison. Mr. Chimp puts his drink down carefully, leans forward, and signs:

T. Edison waves his hand. "Your idea . . . my idea . . . who can say where ideas come from? What matters is what you *make* of an idea."

Mr. Chimp shakes his head slowly. He stands up. He grabs T. Edison's hammock and starts to swing it. Slowly at first. But then faster.

"Hey!" squeaks T. Edison. "OK, slow down. Maybe it *was* both our idea."

Mr. Chimp swings the hammock fast, faster, fastest.

"Hey! Hey! Hey!" T. Edison yells.

Mr. Chimp pushes, flips, spins T. Edison upside down and around and around in complete circles. Pieces of banana muffin fly off the spinning hammock.

“Blaaaaaaaaaaaaaaa!” Edison yells.

“Stop! . . .

“Stop! . . .

“Stop!”

Mr. Chimp jerks the hammock to a quick stop. He looks T. Edison in the eye.

“OK, it was *your* idea.”

Mr. Chimp gives a soft “Hooo Hooo,” and lets the hammock go.

T. Edison sits up in his hammock, dizzy.

The butterfly flaps its wings and lands gently on a little side table.

"But you know what the best part of this whole setup is?"

"Hmmmm?" answers Mr. Chimp, sitting down and twirling his pink drink umbrella.

"We are miles from Midville. And miles from that nosy Frank Einstein and his goober friend and junkyard robots. And there is no way they can mess up my plans this time."

"Hmmm," says Mr. Chimp, finishing his Banana 'n' Ants.

"Exactly," says T. Edison.

Mr. Chimp's phone buzzes.

He checks it and sees his green Security Alert sign.

Mr. Chimp's phone quickly rings with three new alerts.

!

Mr. Chimp's phone quickly rings with three new alerts.

SECURITY PLAN 1 ACTIVATED

SECURITY PLAN 2 ACTIVATED

SECURITY PLAN 3 ACTIVATED

Mr. Chimp pulls on his work hat, and quickly knuckle-walks into the woods.

Edison studies his blueprint. He nods and smiles.

The butterfly flaps its wings.

Edison rolls up the blueprint.

Edison swats the butterfly with a *splat*—

—turning it into a lifeless smudge of black-and-orange-and-white butterfly guts.

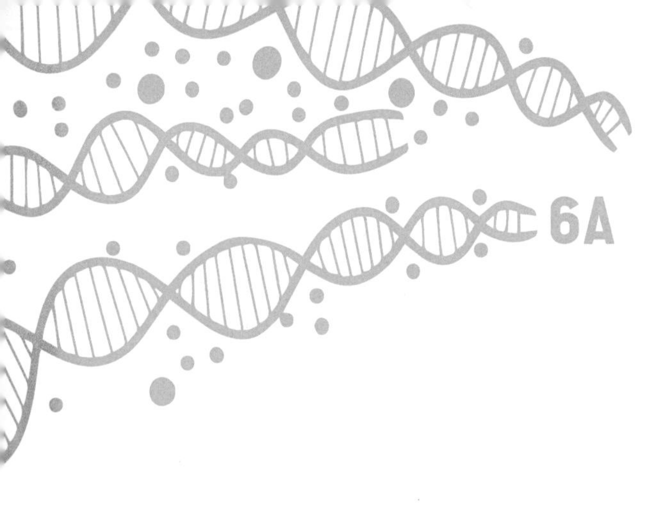

6A

THE MORNING SUN RISES SLOWLY OVER THE CATTAILS AT THE southern end of Lake Darwin.

0930

One human and one small robot sit quietly in a rowboat, drifting with only the wind.

"Look at these crazy monsters!" whispers Watson. "Maybe they are the ones wrecking all the food webs and life cycles!"

Klink confirms Watson's sighting, naming each of the organisms. "Cyclops. Hydra. Water bear (also known as tardigrades). Rotifers . . ."

"Man, I would not want to tangle with them. Yuck."

"Ciliates. Flagellates. Amoebas . . ." continues Klink.

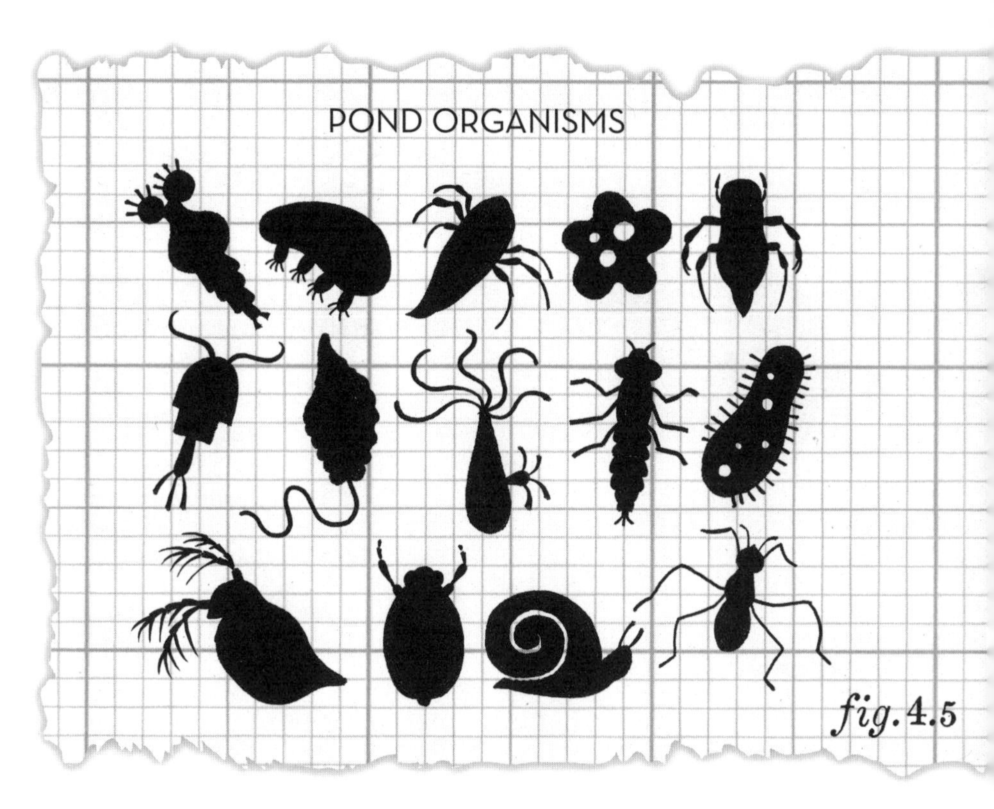

One of the rotifers twirls the hairs around its crown-shaped mouth and clamps a wiggling amoeba with its jaws.

"Yow!" says Watson.

A lumbering water bear chomps a trapped flagellate . . . and sucks the life out of it.

"Tardigrades can survive temperatures as high as 300 degrees Fahrenheit, and as low as minus 450 degrees Fahrenheit. They are also the first-known organisms to survive in space—almost completely unprotected—for ten days."

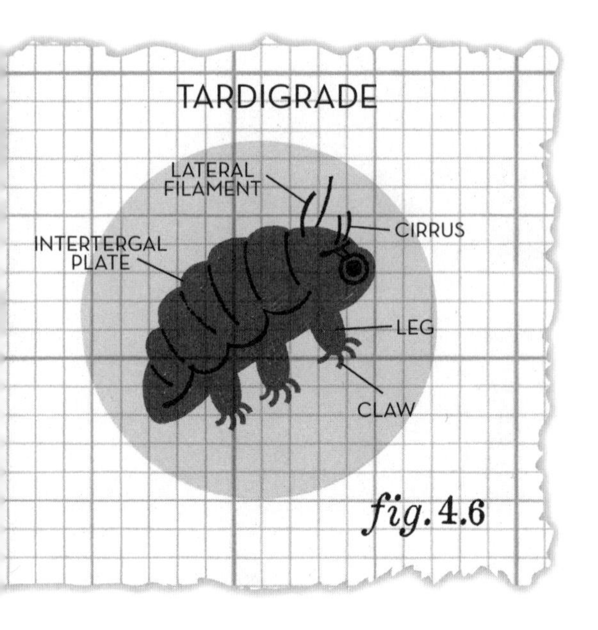

fig. 4.6

"What a beast," says Watson. He looks up from Klink's magnifier attachment. "Good thing he's only half a millimeter long."

"It is survival of the fittest everywhere," says Klink. "Large or small."

Klink extends his fishing-pole attachment.

"Let us also capture, catalog, and observe some of this habitat's cold-blooded aquatic vertebrates."

"You mean—let's fish?"

"Why, yes. What a wonderful, relaxing idea."

Klink casts a purple rubber-worm lure. He leans forward and adjusts the angle on his underwater fish-seeking camera.

Watson casts out a Rapala lure, designed to imitate a wounded minnow.

Klink and Watson watch the fish through Klink's underwater camera attachment.

"Sunfish, perch, bass," says Watson.

"Pike, bluegill, bullhead," spots Klink.

A large, dark figure passes under the boat. It inhales

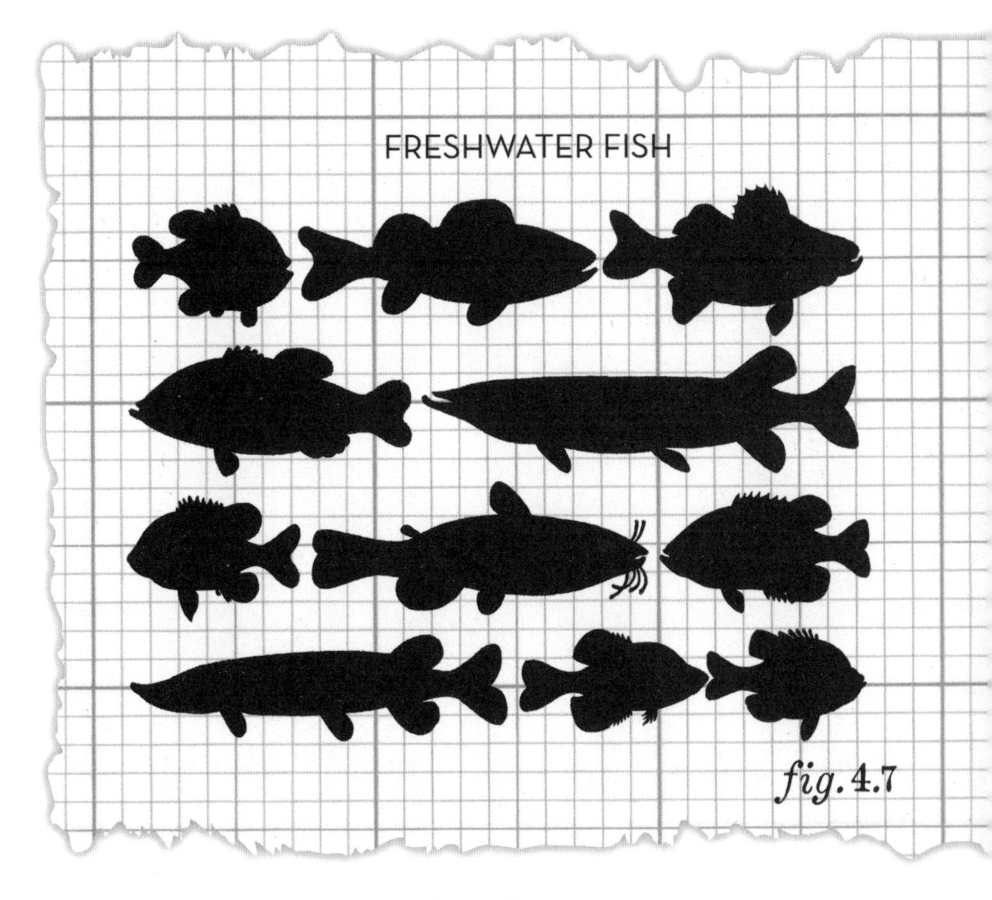

fig. 4.7

Klink's worm and Watson's Rapala, snapping their lines like they were threads.

All the fish scatter in fear.

A freaked-out Watson looks up from the camera viewfinder. "What in the world?"

Klink consults his image databases and calmly reports.

"That appears to have been a plesiosaur."

"You mean, a Loch Ness monster?!"

6B

MEANWHILE, IN THE WOODS, ONE HUMAN AND ONE LARGE robot crash along the hiking trail.

A white-tailed deer jumps over a fallen log and runs off. Two gray squirrels scamper up a walnut tree. A raccoon dives for cover in a blackberry bush. A chipmunk, rabbit, and field mouse race off.

"Klank!" says Frank Einstein. "Try to be a little more quiet. We're supposed to be observing and cataloging the forest habitat. Not scaring it to death."

"Sorry, sorry," beeps Klank.

Turning to talk to Frank, Klank doesn't see the fallen spruce tree in front of him . . . and trips over it with an incredibly loud clanging, crashing metal smash.

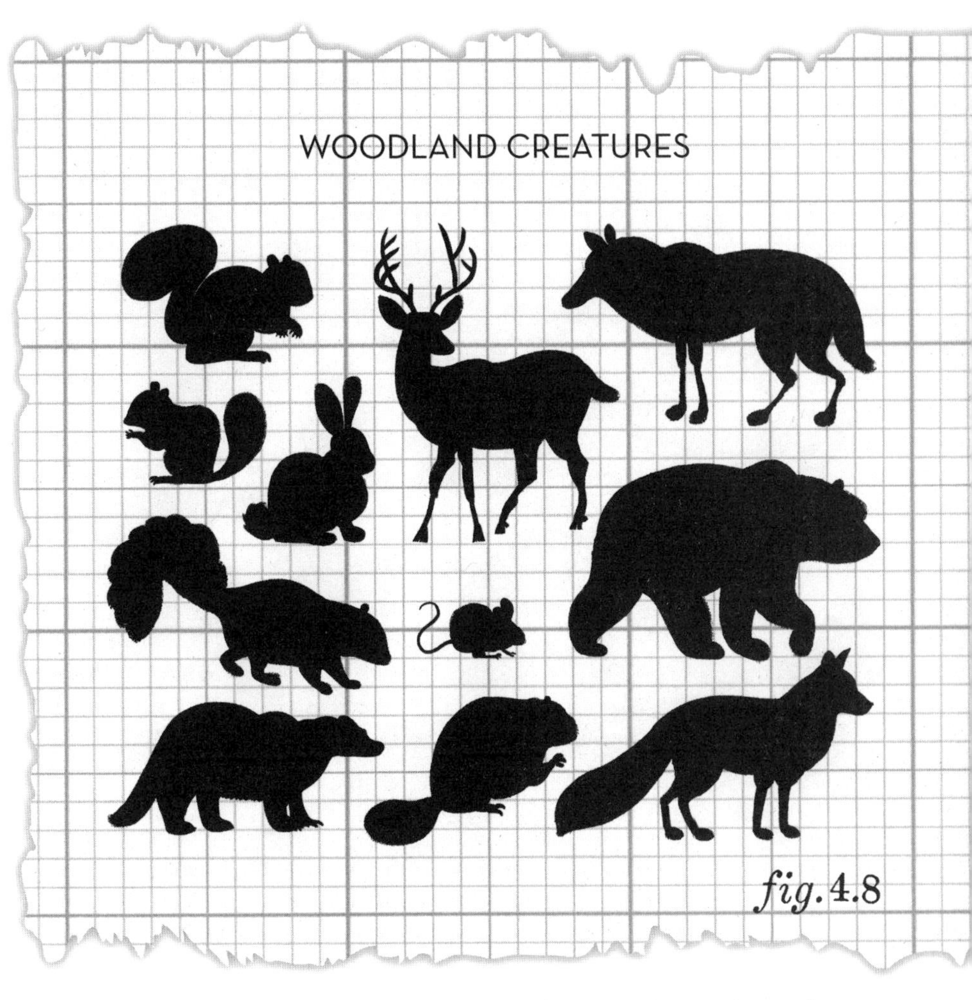

fig. 4.8

Klank's crash sends a deep-red cardinal flying for safety. Followed by two robins, a blue jay, a bunch of sparrows, a red-headed woodpecker, a yellow-rumped warbler, two mourning doves, a red-tailed hawk, a wild turkey, a willow flycatcher, a tufted titmouse, a black-capped chickadee, and one giant great horned owl.

fig. 4.9

"Oooops," says Klank. He rolls over to get back on his feet. And accidentally pokes his Casio keyboard chest. The **3.16 RUMBA** blasts through the woods, scaring off a brown wolf spider, two ladybugs, a Buffalo treehopper, a crane fly, a stink bug, a cloud of mosquitoes, and four grasshoppers.

Klank whacks at his keyboard chest to turn it off, but only manages to change the **RUMBA** to a lively **POLKA**. Which scares off the remaining praying mantis, longhorned beetle, wasp, mayfly, tiger moth, centipede, katydid, jumping spider, pill bug, and three-lined potato beetle.

Klank finally smacks his keyboard off.

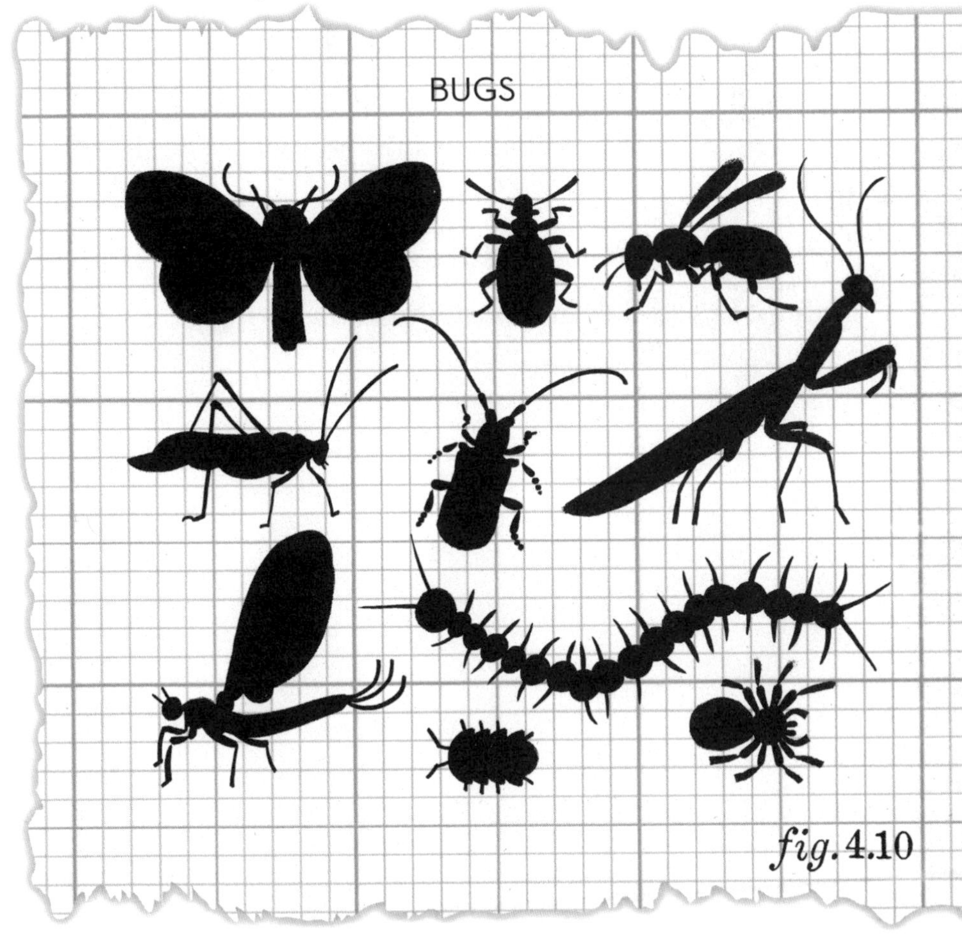

fig. 4.10

"Sorry, sorry, sorry."

Frank Einstein laughs. "Don't be sorry. You just scared up the best list of bird, animal, and insect life."

"I did?"

Klank looks around. He sees something he has seen only in books. He is suddenly afraid. **"B-b-but what kind of life is that?"**

Frank looks up from his notebook. He sees the shape Klank is pointing to. But he doesn't know where he should list the thing slipping between the shadows in the woods.

Because it does not look like animal, bird, or insect life.

"It looks," says Frank Einstein, not believing he is even saying it, "like . . . a ghost."

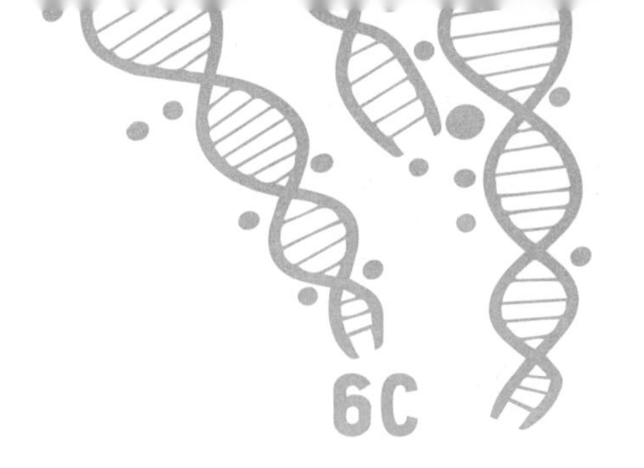

6C

A THIN FIGURE IN WOODLAND CAMOUFLAGE GLIDES PAST THE LAKE, through the woods, and up the faint deer trail alongside the stream that feeds into Lake Darwin.

Grampa Al stops and listens and looks.

With his experienced eye, he reads the woods like a book.

This stream used to be much bigger. Now it's down to a trickle. In the streamside mud—raccoon tracks, duck tracks, the deep imprint of deer hooves.

The raccoon came down to catch the crayfish, frogs, and snails in the stream.

The duck and three ducklings crossed to their nest in the tall grass.

The deer was walking north and jumped over the stream here.

fig. 4.11

Grampa Al moves silently upstream. And that's when he sees a track he has never seen before.

Grampa Al looks quickly all around—then back at the track.

"Whoa, buddy!"

Grampa Al measures the track against his own footprint.

It's not badger or bear or even ape. Too big to be human. But definitely a foot. A very big foot.

Grampa Al follows the tracks of the giant feet across what little is left of the stream, and right up to a towering black woven-metal fence stretching in either direction through the woods, as far as the eye can see.

Grampa Al gives a low, soft whistle.

No water, no insects.

No insects, no frogs.

No frogs, no raccoons . . .

"Now who would mess things up like this?"

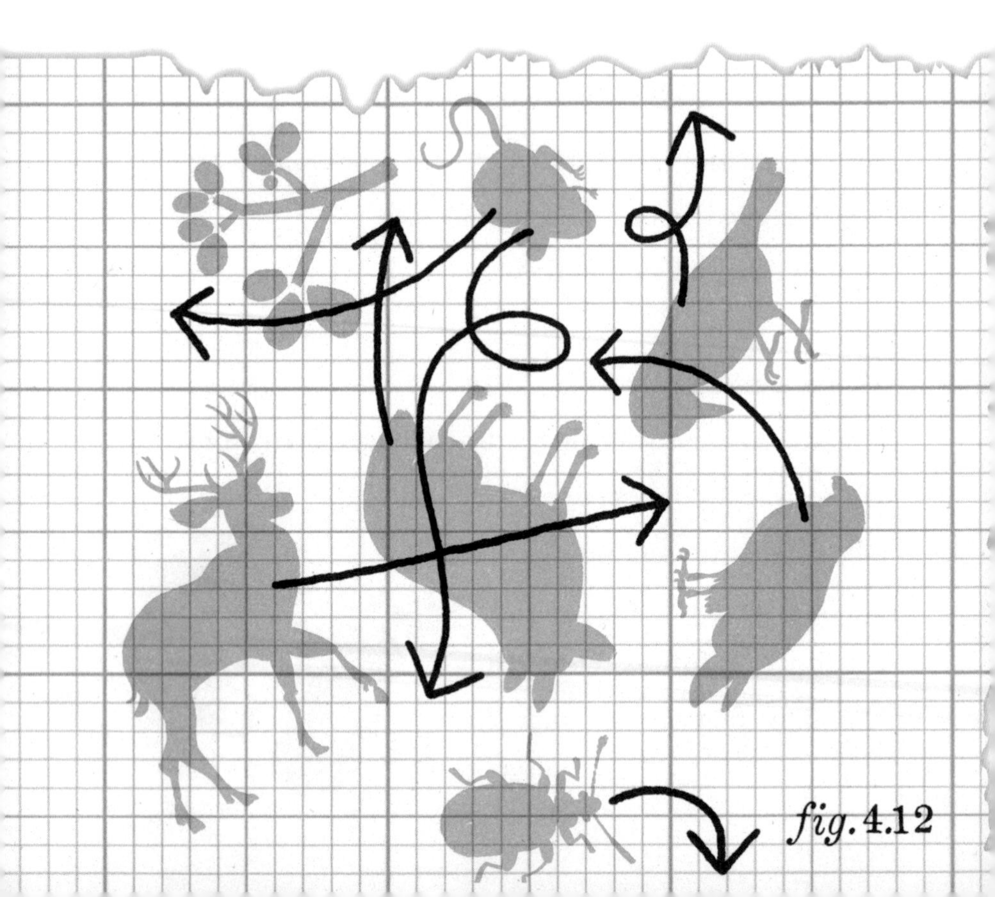

fig. 4.12

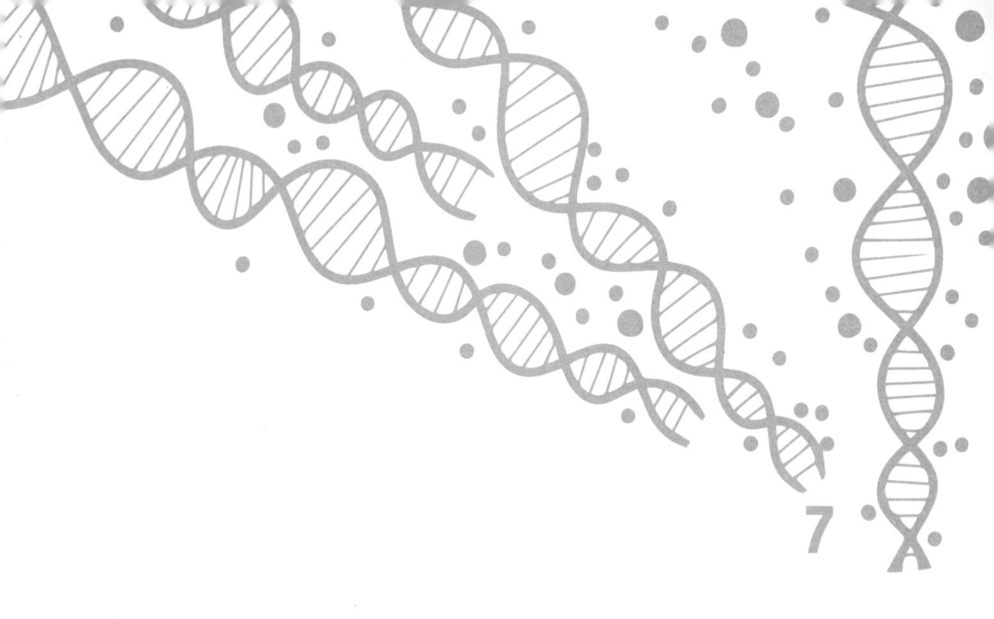

7

"SUMMER SCIENCE SCOUTS!" CALLS THE TRIM SILVER-HAIRED woman in a light-green dress with a dark-green web belt and hiking boots. "Each group has, on the tray in front of you, magnifying glasses, tweezers, toothpicks, and an owl pellet."

"It looks like my cat's hairball," says Anna.

"Disgusting!" says Leslie.

"But very similar to a hairball," says Science Scout leader (as well as Midville Academy principal) Ms. Priscilla. "Can anyone guess what these owl pellets are?"

"Owl food?" says Nicole.

"Good guess . . . but no."

"Owl poop!" yells Jennifer.

"Closer . . . but no."

Janegoodall raises her hand and answers, "It is the parts of anything the owl eats that it can't digest."

"Exactly!" Ms. P. beams. "The owl has a most interesting digestive system—one that separates out whatever it cannot digest, forms it into a ball, and regurgitates it!"

"Completely gross," says Leslie.

"So break apart your pellet and see what it contains."

The six teams of Science Scouts dissect their owl pellets, and check them out under their magnifying glasses.

"Bones!"

"Feathers!"

Scout leader Ms. P. points to her diagram and explains, "Owl beaks are strong enough to tear the flesh of prey, but not strong enough to break bones. So *One*—the swallowed pieces of torn prey travel down the **ESOPHAGUS** to the **PROVENTRICULUS**."

"Teeth! I see little teeth!"

"*Two*—the food travels into the **VENTRICULUS**, and is separated into digestible and not-digestible parts."

"Hair!"

"*Three*—the digestible food passes farther, to the **INTESTINES**.

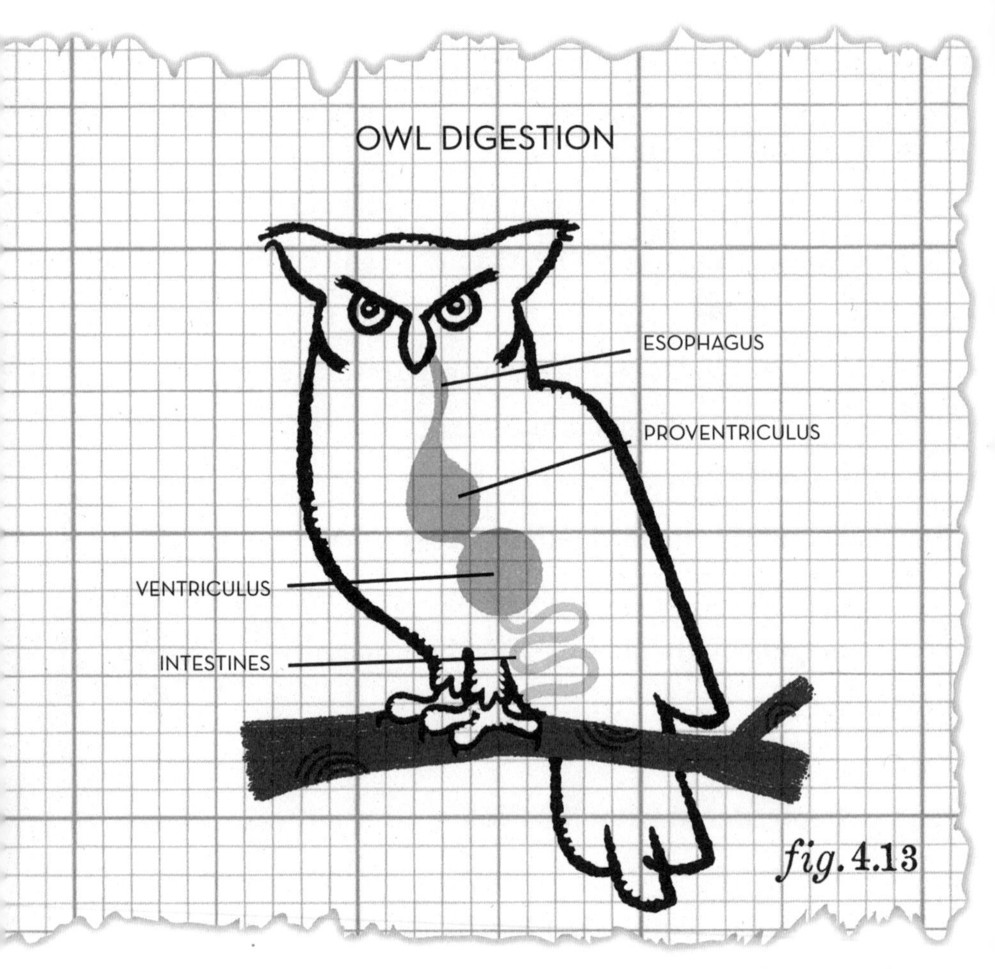

fig. 4.13

But the not-digestible parts are formed into a pellet in the **VENTRICULUS**."

"I think I found a mouse toenail."

"*Four*—the **VENTRICULUS** pushes the pellet back up into the **PROVENTRICULUS**. Where it is sometimes stored for hours."

"I am going to barf my own lunch pellet in a minute," says Leslie.

"And finally, *Five*—" Scout leader Ms. P. thwacks her owl digestion diagram with a flourish. "The owl regurgitates the pellet!"

Anna laughs. "We are picking apart owl puke!"

Scout leader Ms. P. paces around the girls' work tables. "So what do we learn from identifying the contents of the owl pellets?"

Leslie holds her forehead and moans. "That owls are even more disgusting than I ever thought."

Janegoodall holds up a mouse jawbone in her tweezers. "We learn what prey the owl eats."

"Yes." Ms. P. beams again. "So now use your charts to

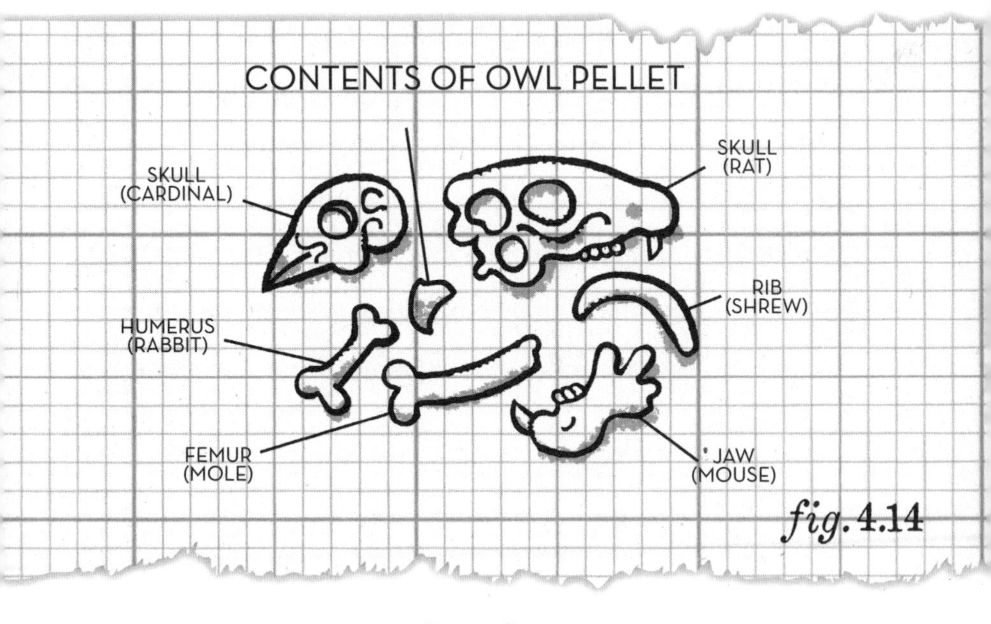

fig. 4.14

identify individual bones. See how many different types you can find."

"I've got a bird hip!"

"Oh this is definitely a rat foot."

"I think I've got a shrew leg."

"Yes, yes, yes," says Ms. P.

Janegoodall and her partner arrange their findings on a sheet of paper.

"This is great, Ms. P.," says Janegoodall. "But since we are out in the woods, couldn't we learn more about owls by observing them in their natural habitat?"

Ms. P. smiles and nods. "Spoken like a true scientist, Janegoodall. And an excellent idea. Which is why we are hiking to Darwin Park for our Owl-Spotting Sleepover!"

"Oh, great," says Leslie, frowning at Janegoodall. "So now we get to sleep in those nasty tents . . . and have owls puke on us."

"Yes!" says Janegoodall. She quickly packs her Swiss Army knife, her chocolate-cherry-nut energy bars, and her binoculars in her camouflage backpack. "Time for some real fieldwork!"

8

WATSON DROPS HIS FISHING GEAR IN THE CORNER OF THE Einstein Labs and HQ tent. "You are not going to believe what we saw in the water!"

Klink pulls a photo out of his printer port and places it on the wooden campsite table.

Frank, Klank, and Grampa Al gather around to take a look.

"Oh yes, we are going to believe it," says Klank. **"Because in the woods, we saw a ghost!"**

"Or something that *looked* like a ghost," Frank corrects Klank.

"And just as strange up the stream . . ." Grampa Al plops a plaster cast of one very large, almost human-looking foot on the pine table.

"Bigfoot!" says Watson.

"And a Loch Ness monster?" asks Frank.

"And a ghost?" beeps Klank.

"All in one place?" says Watson.

"Very suspicious," concludes Frank.

Grampa Al unfolds a map of Darwin Park and spreads it out. "And even more suspicious when you look at where our three sightings happened. Here, here, and here. All on the northern edge of Darwin Park.

"*And* . . . the tracks end at a gigantic fence surrounding Park Area 51."

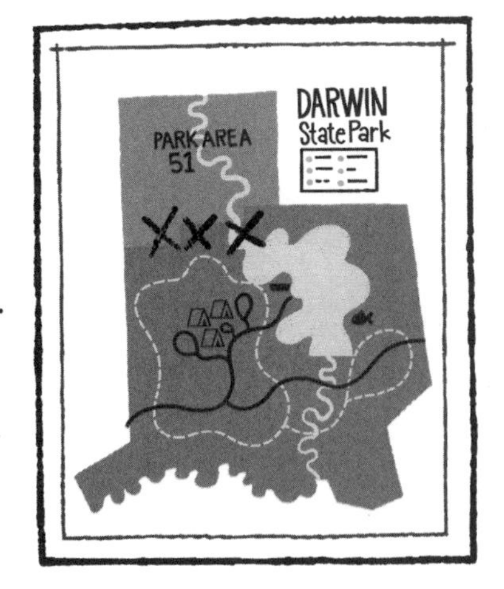

Frank rubs his head and thinks. "It may sound like the plot of a cheesy cartoon, but somebody, or something, does not want us to get into Area 51."

"OK," says Klank. **"I will pack our gear and we will go away."**

"Oh no!" says Watson. "Not when we have a chance to catch the Loch Ness monster *and* Bigfoot *and* a ghost."

Klank squeezes his metal vegetable-strainer head. **"That would be fun. But we cannot break any rules."**

"You are right to always follow your Three Laws of Robotics," says Grampa Al. "But sometimes humans give orders that shouldn't be followed—like this order to keep out."

Klank tries to think about this. But it makes no sense to his robot brain. He tries thinking again, then suddenly starts ringing like an old-fashioned telephone.

RING-RING. RING-RING. RING-RING.

"Well," says Klink, "would someone please answer him?"

"Why is Klank ringing?" asks Watson.

"I figured we might need improved communication out here in the woods," says Frank, "so I wired Klank with a satellite phone."

RING-RING. RING-RING. RING-RING.

Frank lifts a flap under Klank's arm and picks up an

old-fashioned pay phone receiver. A satellite antenna extends out of Klank's head.

"Hello, Einstein Mobile Laboratories."

"Hey, champ!"

"Oh, hi, Dad."

"Guess where we are?"

"Olduvai Gorge, next to the Serengeti National Park in Tanzania in Africa?"

"Wow, great guess."

"I gave this phone a computer-map display," says Frank. "And . . . you told me and Grampa where you and Mom were going, remember?"

"Ohhhhhhhh, right, right," says Dad Einstein. "And you should see this place. Amazing! This is where scientists found fossils and stone tools from what we think are the earliest human species that modern humans evolved from."

"Mary and Louis Leakey," says Frank.

"You what?"

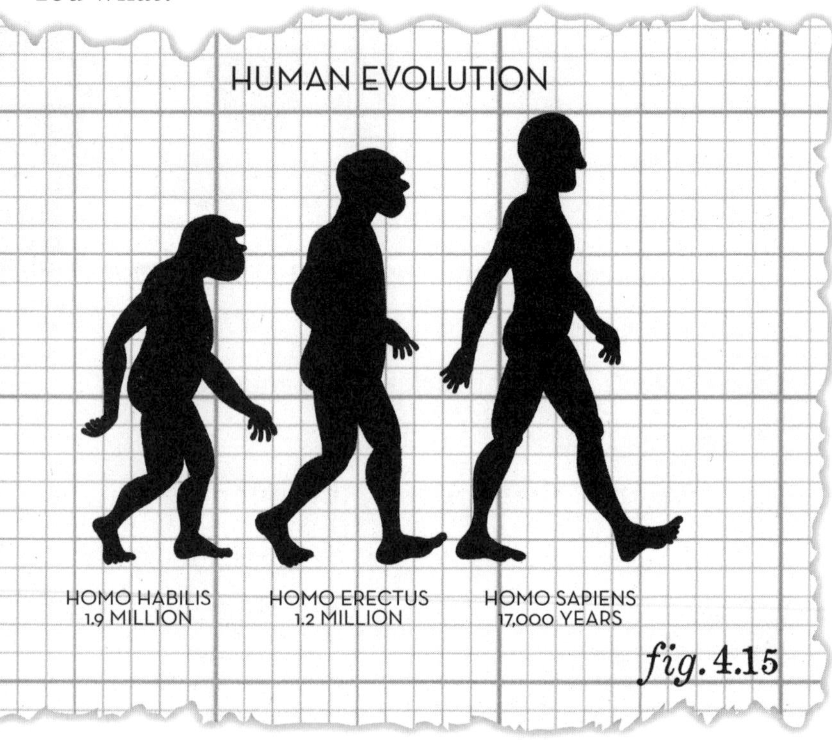

fig. 4.15

"Those were the scientists. Mary and Louis Leakey."

"Oh, right, right. Here's your mom."

"Hello, darling. We were just thinking about you. And Grampa Al. Did you remember to pack your bug spray and sunscreen?"

"Hi, Mom. And yep. We packed everything. Because we packed Klink. And he is completely outfitted with every attachment we could need."

"That is so nice that you all get to take a relaxing camping trip together. It must be so nice and quiet."

Frank slides the picture of the Loch Ness monster and the cast of Bigfoot across the table. "Uhhhh . . . yeah. We are mostly relaxing. Checking out all of the wildlife. All Interconnected Life."

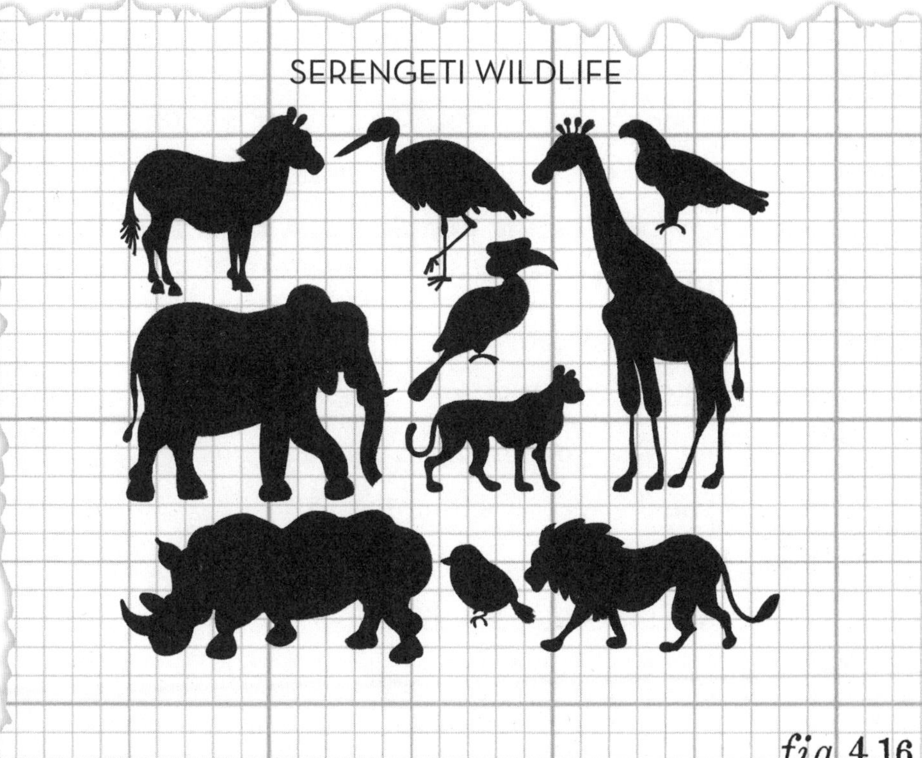

"Oh my goodness, the wildlife here is absolutely wonderful. Amazing what variety of species have evolved. Lions, cheetahs, giraffes, zebras—"

"And eagles and storks and hornbills and a yellow-rumped tinkerbird!" Dad shouts in the background.

"And rhinos and elephants—"

"Oooooooo!" beeps Klank. **"Elephants! Hellloooooo, Mrs. Einstein. Do you know why elephants have flat feet?"**

"Hello, Klank. No, I don't think I know. Why do elephants have flat feet?"

"Noooooooooo," says Klink. "Do not let him do this!" Klink wheels out of the HQ tent as fast as he can.

Klank lights up. **"From jumping out of trees! Ha. Ha. Ha. Ha. Ha. Ha. Ha. Ha."**

Frank shakes his head.

"OK! Bye, Mom. Bye, Dad."

"Bye, Frank. Give your grampa a big hug for us."

"We got you this nice evolution T-shirt!"

Frank hangs up the Klank phone.

Klank's satellite antenna retracts.

Frank scratches his head—like he always does when he is thinking. "Evolution . . . different forms of life . . . I think I might have an idea, Watson."

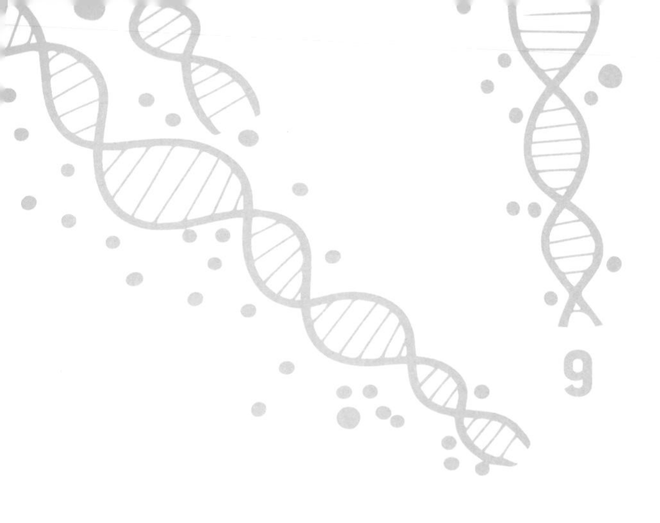

9

"THERE!" WHISPERS JANEGOODALL. SHE STEADIES HER BINOCULARS on a large dark-brown shape high in a tall maple tree on the edge of a field. She sharpens the focus, and spots the distinctive ear tufts of feathers that give the big bird its name.

"A great horned owl."

The owl turns its head left, right, 270 degrees in either direction, almost all the way around. It uses its supersensitive hearing to pinpoint a sound below.

Janegoodall, Anna, and

Leslie unconsciously hold their breath, freezing as still and quiet as possible.

Covered by the deep grass in the field, feeling safe from any predator, a gray squirrel chews, just a little too noisily, on an acorn.

Giant yellow owl eyes zero in on the faint motion of the grass. The ultrapredator leans forward, pushes off with its knife-sharp taloned claws, and dives headfirst off the tree branch.

The squirrel drops the acorn.

The owl spreads its large wings and flaps once, making virtually no noise because of the very particular shape of its feathers.

So the squirrel never even hears its end coming.

BAM!

Owl talons rip through the grass, break the squirrel's

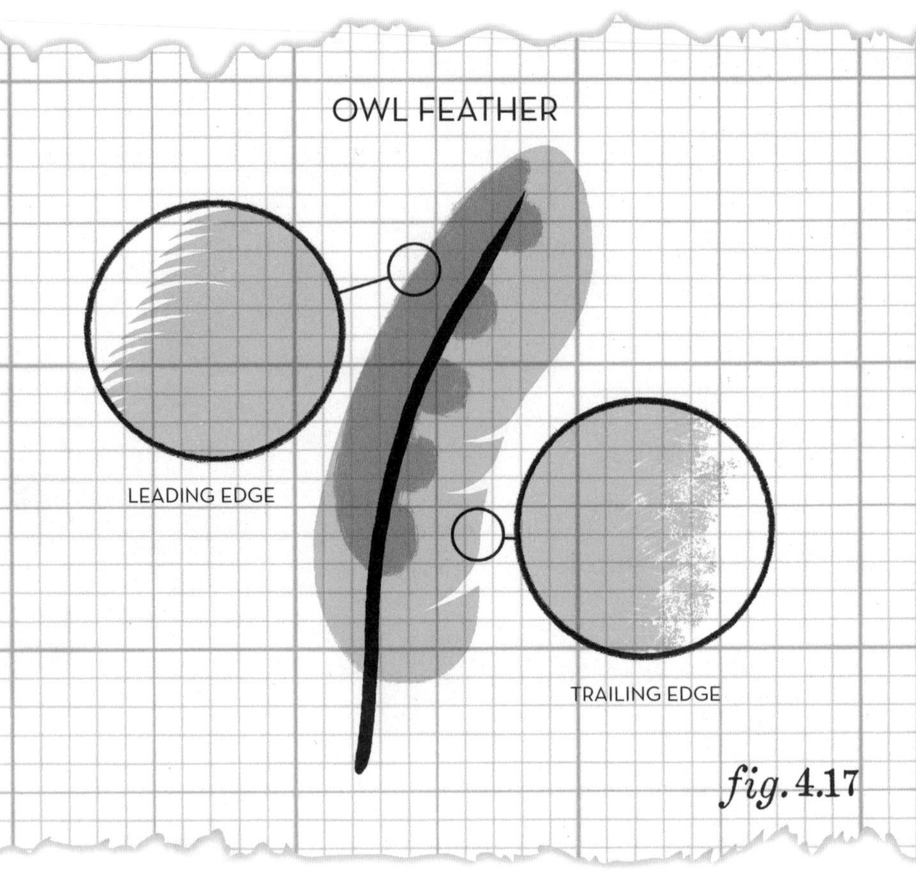

neck bones. Owl beak spears squirrel skull, rips apart squirrel flesh, swallows squirrel almost whole. The great horned owl looks left, right, and flies off into the woods.

"Wooooooowwwww," says Janegoodall. She lowers her binoculars. "What a predator!"

"It never even made a sound!" says Anna.

"Let's see if there are any old owl pellets," says Janegoodall.

The three Science Scouts walk over to the base of the big maple tree.

“Now I am *definitely* going to upchuck my own lunch pellet,” answers Leslie. “Let’s get back to camp.”

Janegoodall and Anna scour the ground for owl pellets. No luck.

Janegoodall follows a faint path deeper into the woods. “Maybe over here.”

“Come onnnnn, you guys. I’m hungry.”

“OK, OK . . . whoaaa. Hey! What is this?”

Janegoodall and Anna slip between the trees to check out a towering black woven-metal fence, almost invisible in the shifting light, but impossible to get over or around.

Anna reads a small green sign.

This only makes Anna more curious. “What could be in there?”

Anna shakes the fence.

10

BBBZZZZZZZZZZZ GOES THE Nature Good! INTRUDER ALERT.

Mr. Chimp puts away his giant rubber Bigfoot.

Mr. Chimp checks his Nature Good security cam. He sees three small figures in Section 33.3 shake the fence again.

Bbbbzzzzzzzzzz!

Mr. Chimp zooms in on the image. He sees three girls dressed in green uniforms.

Mr. Chimp checks his security cam. He zooms in on Grampa Al.

The Nature Good! Intruder Alert flashes again.

Mr. Chimp holds his chin, taps one leathery chimp finger against his front tooth, and thinks.

Mr. Chimp comes up with two more great Security Plans.

Mr. Chimp selects two metal coat hangers from his Security Storeroom.

Mr. Chimp hacks into Grampa Al's phone and dials a Code Red.

Mr. Chimp sits back. And smiles. Sort of.

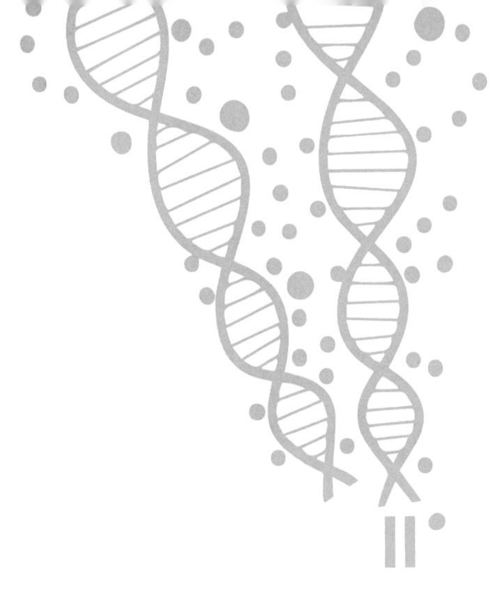

11

YOU FELLAS SURE YOU'LL BE OK FOR ONE NIGHT WITHOUT ME?” asks Grampa Al.

Frank looks up from the sketches and plans and parts and pieces on the camp table in front of him. He checks Watson, Klink, and Klank, who are already hard at work on their assignments.

“Oh yeah. We've got plenty to do here.”

“And we've got Klink and Klank to protect us,” adds Watson.

Grampa Al climbs into his Fix It! shop truck and fires up the old vehicle.

“I don't like leaving you. But I got this Code Red call just now. And I've got to go. I'll be back tomorrow.”

Frank waves. “We won’t do anything you wouldn’t do.”

“That’s what worries me,” says Grampa Al, with a smile. He puts the Fix It! shop truck in gear, and roars off down the dirt camp road.

Watson shuffles through his pile of pictures and charts and diagrams. “What is all this, Einstein? And how is it going to help us get inside that Area 51?”

Frank rubs his head with both hands.

“Here’s what I’m thinking.”

VARIETY OF LIFE

. . . writes Frank, with a piece of charcoal, on the side of the tent.

"Klink! Projector, please."

Klink swivels his webcam eye around. "This better be for something good. And not a waste of my superior skills and talents."

Frank ignores Klink's crabby comment. "How many different species of living things are there on Earth?"

Klink's glass head dome lights up. "Yes! Now this is my kind of question. Research! Information! Organization!"

Klink hums for three seconds, searching his databases. He flips on his high-intensity projector and displays a chart on the side of the tent.

"It is almost impossible to know how many species exist on Earth. But biologists estimate there are about ten million.

"Scientists organize all of these living things into five, and sometimes six, groups . . . called kingdoms.

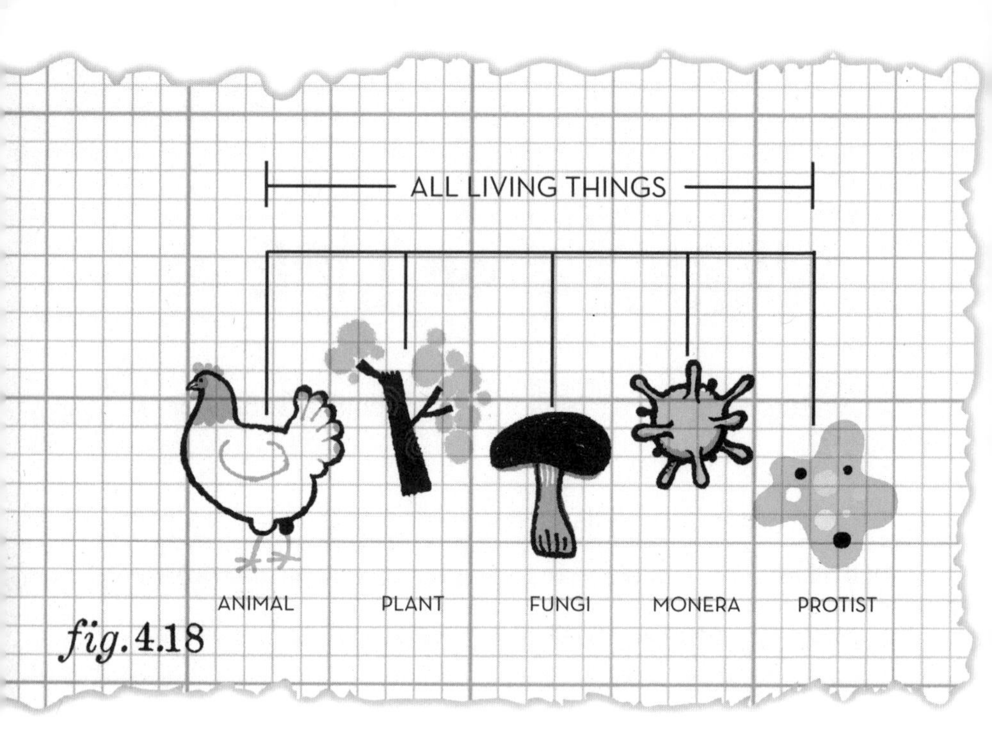

*fig.*4.18

Animal kingdom. Plant kingdom. Fungi kingdom. Monera kingdom. Protist kingdom."

"Great," says Frank.

"Shall I explain the characteristics of each kingdom?"

"Maybe later," says Frank.

"Awwwwwww."

"Watson! What did you find on how Earth got all these different species?"

EVOLUTION OF LIFE

. . . writes Frank, on the tent, next to **VARIETY OF LIFE**.

"Scientists have calculated that our planet Earth formed about 4.6 billion years ago," says Watson.

"The first signs of life, simple cells, have been found as fossils from 3.5 billion years ago.

"Multicelled life, one billion years ago.

"Fish, 500 million years ago.

"Land plants, 475 million years ago.

"Insects, 400 million years ago.

"Reptiles and dinosaurs, 250 million years ago."

Klank interrupts, **"Ooooh I love dinosaurs!"**

"Mammals, that we humans are part of, 200 million years ago," Watson continues.

"And then the line of our human ancestors.

"Primates, 60 million years ago.

"Great apes, 20 million years ago.

"The genus *Homo*, meaning man, 2.5 million years ago.

"Modern humans, *Homo sapiens* (wise man), only 200,000 years ago."

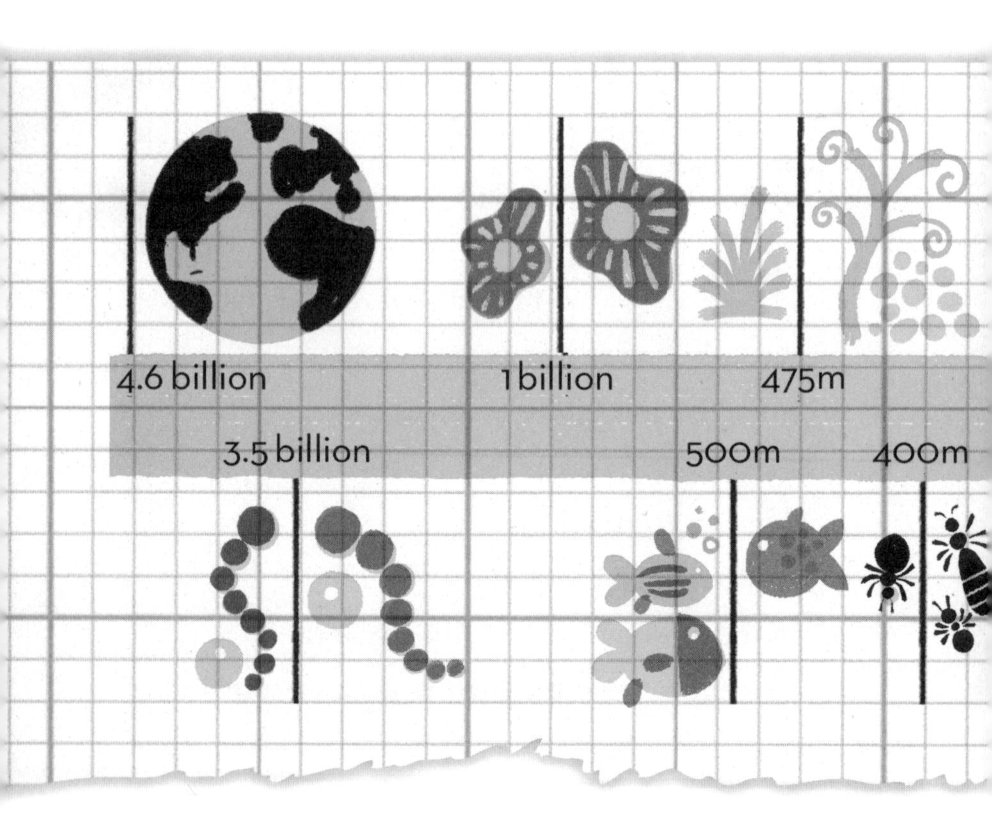

Klink projects Watson's timeline on the tent:

Watson studies the **VARIETY OF LIFE** chart and the **EVOLUTION OF LIFE** timeline . . . and scratches his head.

"This is all pretty amazing. But how is it supposed to help us?"

Frank Einstein nods. "Two more important pieces."

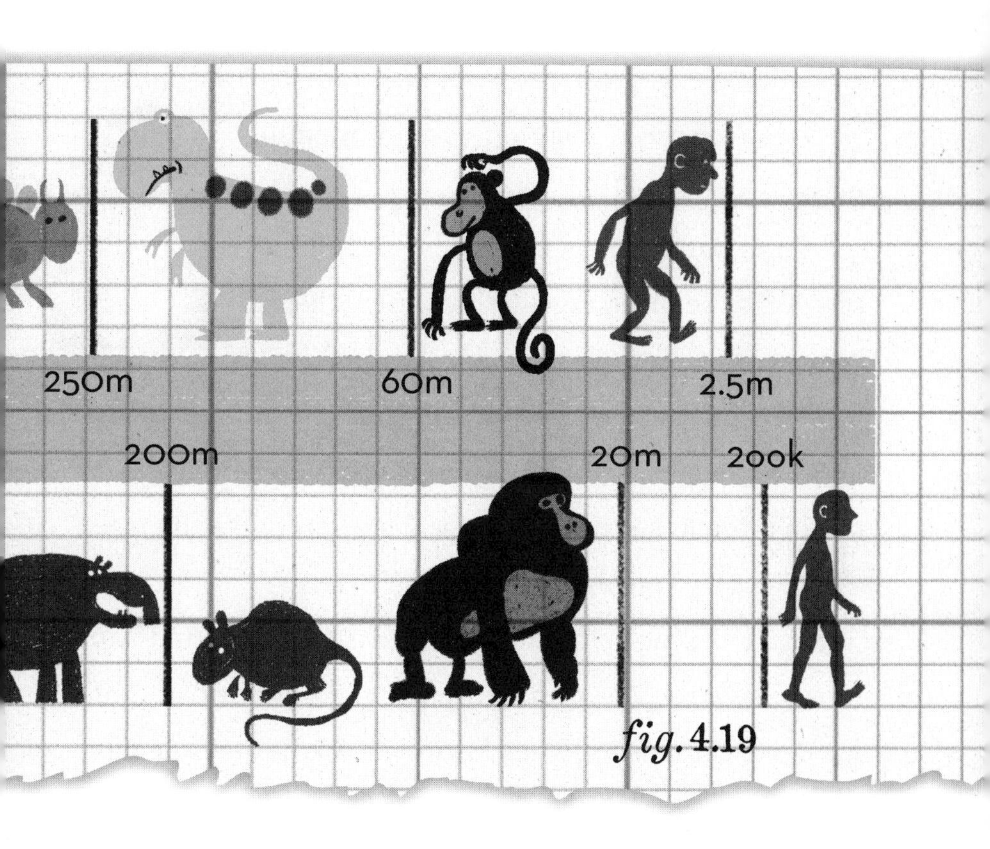

fig. 4.19

ORIGIN OF SPECIES

. . . writes Frank, on the tent.

"In 1859, Charles Darwin wrote up his idea that all living things evolved from those first simple cells."

Klink flashes up an illustration of Charles Darwin.

"Darwin figured out that evolution could happen by natural selection.

"Plants and animals changed over billions of years by small changes in individuals being passed down to their offspring."

"Like I changed my head that time I blew up."

Frank laughs. "Not like that. More like the dark moth on this tree. It survives because it's colored like the tree."

"So?" says Watson.

"So a white moth on the same tree is easily spotted—and more likely to get eaten. More dark moths survive. They have more offspring. They become a whole new species."

Watson still looks confused.

"So how does all of this help us get inside Park Area 51?"

MECHANISM OF EVOLUTION

. . . writes Frank, on the tent, next to the other three headings.

"All things evolve and change from one form to another.

"A cell can evolve into a plant.

"A wormlike animal can evolve into a whale.

"Humans evolved from monkey-type animals."

"**Which explains a lot about you humans,**" says Klink.

Frank ignores Klink's wisecrack. "And all of these crazy changes are made possible by DNA molecules inside every living thing!"

A single cricket gives one chirp.

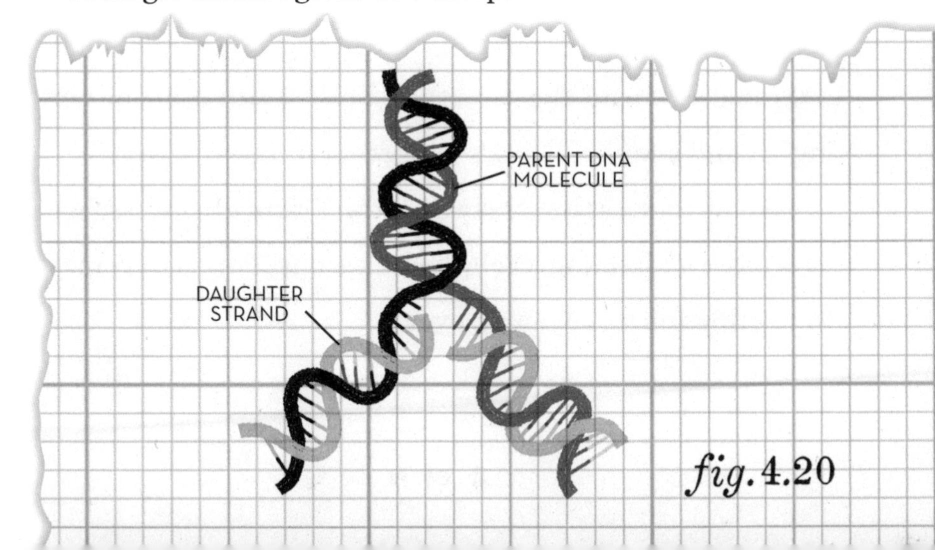

fig. 4.20

"Uhhhh . . . great," says Watson. "But I'm still not getting how this helps us invent anything to get us into Park Area 51."

Frank smiles. He explains what to him is perfectly obvious.

"So nothing human can possibly get into Park Area 51. But what about something *not human*?"

"Maybe . . ." says Watson.

"Evolution takes a long time. All the DNA unzipping and reforming and natural selection takes millions and millions of years. But what if we could hop around the process? What if we could superspeed evolve and blast from one species to another?"

Watson looks at all the diagrams about species, evolution, and DNA on the makeshift Wall of Science.

"Are you kidding?"

Frank holds up the wrestling belt. "With a bit of wiring . . . and a few of Klink's gadgets . . ."

Watson looks at the crazy smile on Frank Einstein's face.

"You aren't kidding. Well, count me out. This is too crazy. No testing for me. No way, ever."

Klank is still thinking about evolution. And dinosaurs.

Klank asks, **"Why did the dinosaur stand on the marshmallow?"**

"No!" says Klink. "No, no, no!"

"So it wouldn't sink in the hot chocolate!"

"What?!"

Klink's head glows red.

"No!"

Klink's circuits overheat.

"Eeeeeeeeeeeee!"

Klink's headbulb explodes with a sad *pffft!*

CHICKEN FARMER
CHICKEN FARMER

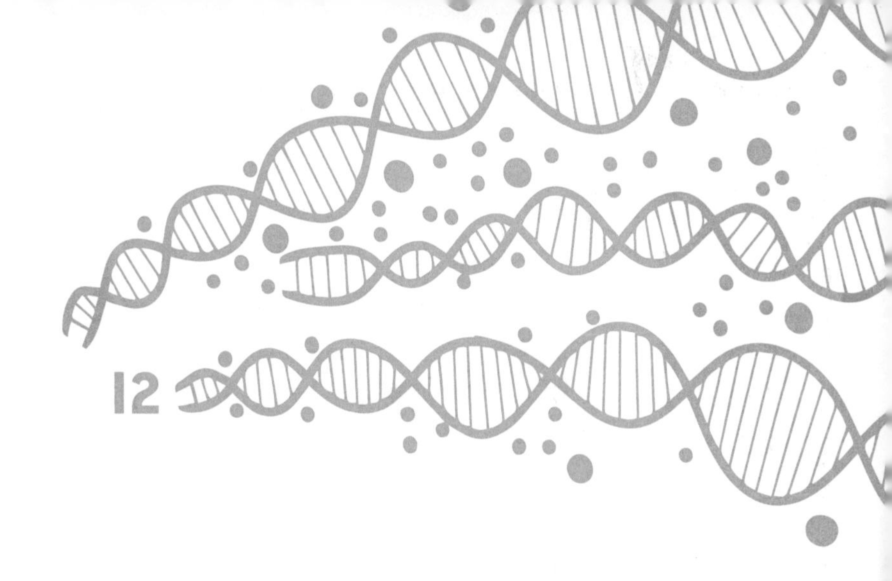

A SMILING MR. CHIMP SWINGS FROM BRANCH TO BRANCH. He drops onto the roof of the Nature Good Edison factory building. He opens the roof hatch, and climbs down the ladder to the Nature Good Lounge.

T. Edison sits in his Edison Lounge Chair, eating Cheezy Puffs, looking out over the Nature Good factory line, and reading his *Chicken Farmer* magazine.

"Where have you been, you lazy monkey? We've got work to do here! I don't know why I even hired you. I have to do everything—inventing, building, dominating nature, and bending it to my will."

Mr. Chimp signs:

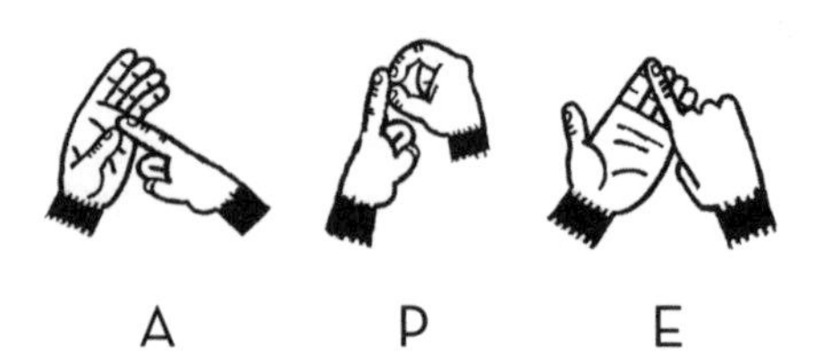

T. Edison waves one hand. “Yes, yes, yes. I know—you are not a monkey. You are an ape. I don’t know why you are so sensitive about that. Who cares? Do I look like I care? Ask me if I care.”

Mr. Chimp signs:

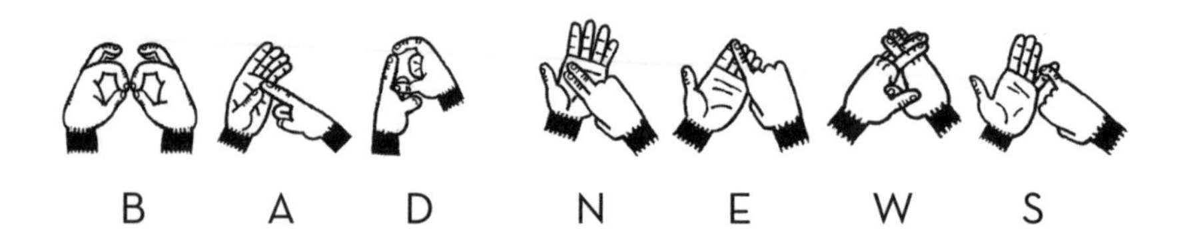

“No kidding. It’s bad news what I have to put up with. It’s bad news I have to work so hard turning free water into bottles of profit. It’s bad news no one is as smart as me. Tell me something I don’t know.”

T. Edison cranks a lever. The water bottle line speeds up.

Mr. Chimp shows T. Edison a security cam photo on his phone.

T. Edison chews another handful of Cheezy Puffs and leans forward.

"Science Scouts? What are Science Scouts doing snooping around here? Scare them off!"

Mr. Chimp nods.

Mr. Chimp shows T. Edison another photo.

"Old man hunting? Same thing. Scare him away!"

Mr. Chimp zooms the camera in on the hunter's face.

"What? Oh no. Is that Grampa Einstein? The grandfather of that pest, Frank Einstein?"

Mr. Chimp nods yes.

"Get him out of here!"

Mr. Chimp nods. Mr. Chimp clicks on a live webcam.

T. Edison drops his bag of Cheezy Puffs.

"Nooooooooooo! Two robots? And that Watson kid? Don't tell me it's . . . Frank Einstein out here too!"

T. Edison stamps his foot on the bag of Cheezy Puffs, crushing the last of the "cheese-flavored cheese snacks" into a neon orange powder.

"Unleash *all* our monster tricks! Freak them out! Get them out of there!"

Mr. Chimp studies the webcam. He watches Frank Einstein and Watson and Klink and Klank working on something.

Mr. Chimp nods to himself. He may be a chimp, but he is no fool. He's already taken care of the old man. He will take care of the Science Scouts tonight. But he knows he will not be able to scare off a scientist/inventor/genius like Frank Einstein with just any old scare tactic.

So Mr. Chimp comes up with a much better plan.

T. Edison stamps his foot again.

Mr. Chimp pulls his **SECURITY** hat back on, climbs up the ladder, and out the rooftop hatch.

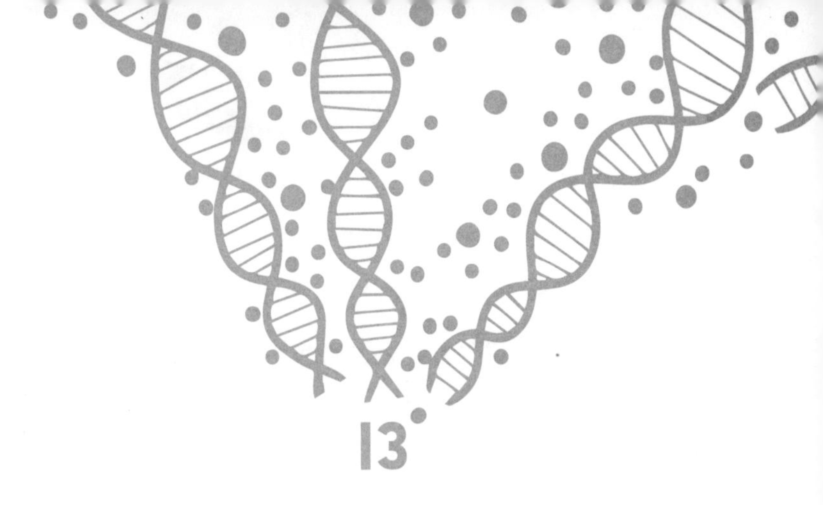

13

SO THE TWO OF THEM DRIVE UP TO A DESERTED SPOT IN THE WOODS and park the car," says Anna.

The circle of summer Science Scouts moves a little closer to the campfire.

Leslie's eyes bug out. "Oh, that is *not* a good idea."

A great horned owl (in fact—the exact same great horned owl the scouts saw earlier in the day) hoots in the quiet dusk.

"And then . . . just as the cute boy is about to turn off the car, the radio says: '*Emergency bulletin. A dangerous killer has escaped. Lock your doors and windows.*'"

"Ohhhhhhh," says Janegoodall.

Anna leans in. “The girl hears this and she says, ‘We have to get out of here. Right now.’”

“‘Yikes!’ says the boy. ‘The killer could be right outside.’”

“‘*And one more thing,*’ says the radio. ‘*The escaped killer has a hook for a hand.*’”

“Eeeeeeeeeee!” Leslie squeaks. “Get out of there!”

It’s a warm night. But everyone moves closer to the fire.

“‘Let’s get out of here,’ says the boy. ‘But before we go, let’s at least kiss once.’”

"No no no!" says Leslie. "Get out of there *now*!"

"The girl really does want to kiss the boy, but she is worried about the killer. So she says, 'OK, one kiss. Then let's roll up the windows and get out of here.'

"They kiss. They roll up the windows. And they drive off."

Leslie uncovers her eyes. "Are they OK? No one got killed? Or hooked? Phew."

Anna looks around the fire. She lowers her voice. "The boy drives them back down into town. He parks the car at her house. He gets out to open her door. And that's when he sees it . . ."

Anna pauses.

"Sees what? What?!"

"Trapped in the rolled-up window. Hanging there with bloody bits dripping from it. A *hook*!"

Everyone screams.

The great horned owl, startled by the sudden night-piercing noise, flies off.

In the top branches of a pin oak tree, out of the reach of the flickering firelight, Mr. Chimp nods. He pulls out a wire coat hanger—and bends it in half to extend the hook.

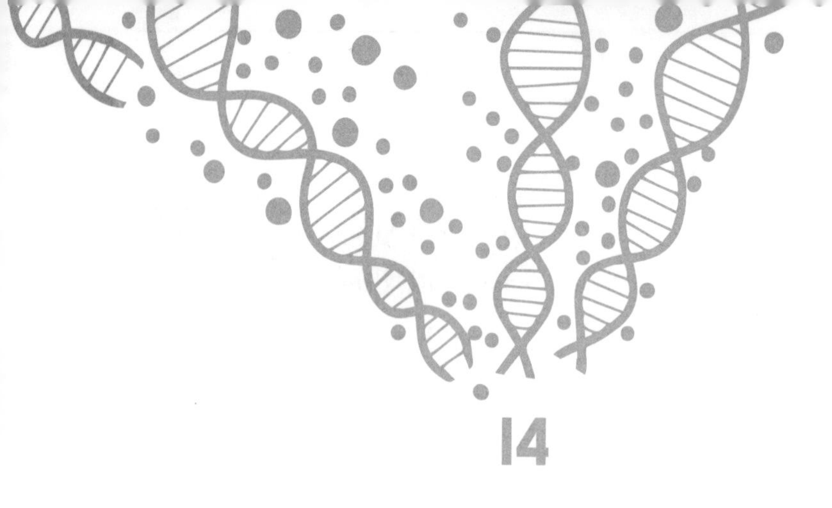

14

KLINK FOLDS AWAY HIS ELECTRON MICROSCOPE ATTACHMENT. "All systems check."

Klank splits one last log with his ax-hand. **"All firewood chopped."**

Frank Einstein picks up the championship-wrestling belt. It has some interesting new additions—a compass, a corkscrew, a gold disk, a hyperspeed DNA splitter/re-zipper, and the control buttons of Klank's TV remote.

"What in the world?" says Watson.

Frank announces, "Laaaadieeeees and gentlemeeeeeen-nnnn! Frank Einstein Laboratories presents! Our newest! Our biggest! Our craziest invention yet!" Frank holds his invention overhead. "The EeeeeeeevoBlaster Belt!"

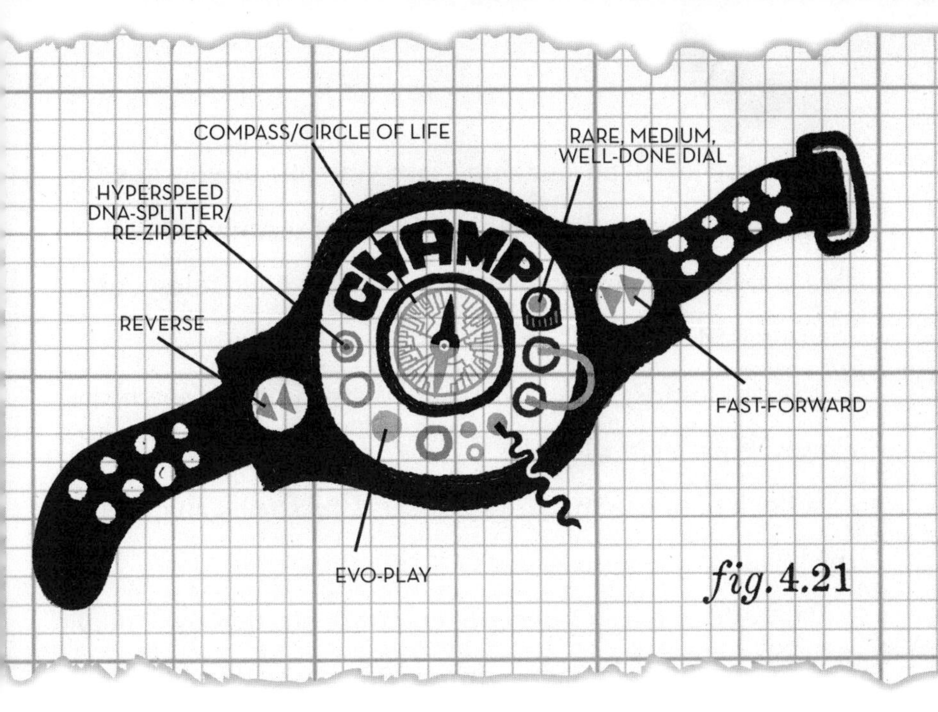

*fig.*4.21

Klank pushes a group of three keys on his keyboard all at once. The noise of a cheering crowd blasts out of his speaker: *"Wooooo! Yeah! Allll right!"*

Klink swivels his eye on Klank, and shakes his glass head. "You do not even know what it does."

Klank thinks about this for a minute. **"Well . . . no . . . But it sure looks cool!"** Klank blasts another crowd cheer. *"Wooooo! Yeah! Allll right!"*

Watson puts down his new fishing rod invention. "It does look very cool."

Frank slings the gold belt over his shoulder. "Come on, I'll show you what it does. This is going to be amazing."

“I’m sure it will be amazing,” says Watson, nervously. “But remember—I am only watching. I am not testing any part of this craziness. I am safely working on my new Telescoping Fishing Rod.”

Klank clomps, Klink rolls, and Watson walks down the campsite path after Frank.

A flock of house sparrows (*Passer domesticus*) chatters in the bushes.

Three blue jays (*Cyanocitta cristata*), startled by a small furry-something swinging through the trees, squawk their alarm call and burst into flight.

Frank explains as they walk down the trail.

“It’s called the EvoBlaster Belt because it will allow us to blast all around evolution—a process that takes millions of years—in seconds.”

“That’s nuts,” says Watson.

Frank kneels down at the edge of the meadow. He adjusts the EvoBlaster Belt controls.

“No no no. It makes perfect sense. Remember Darwin’s original idea of All Connected Life? Darwin saw it like branches of a tree.

"But the more we learned about species, the bigger and more complicated the tree of life got.

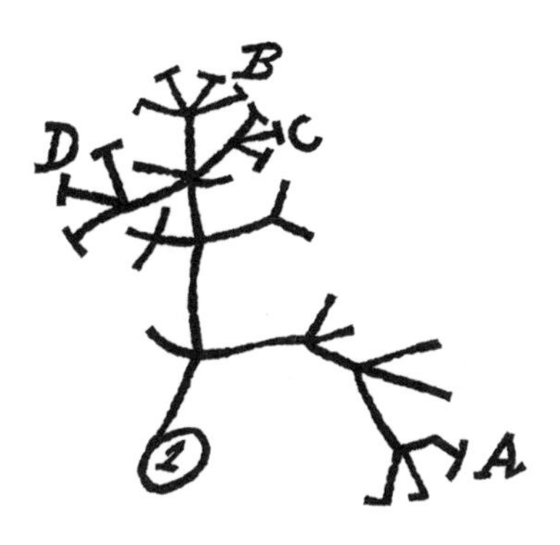

"And now we know about so many millions of species in the whole history of the earth, that the tree of life has turned into a giganto Connected Circle of Life."

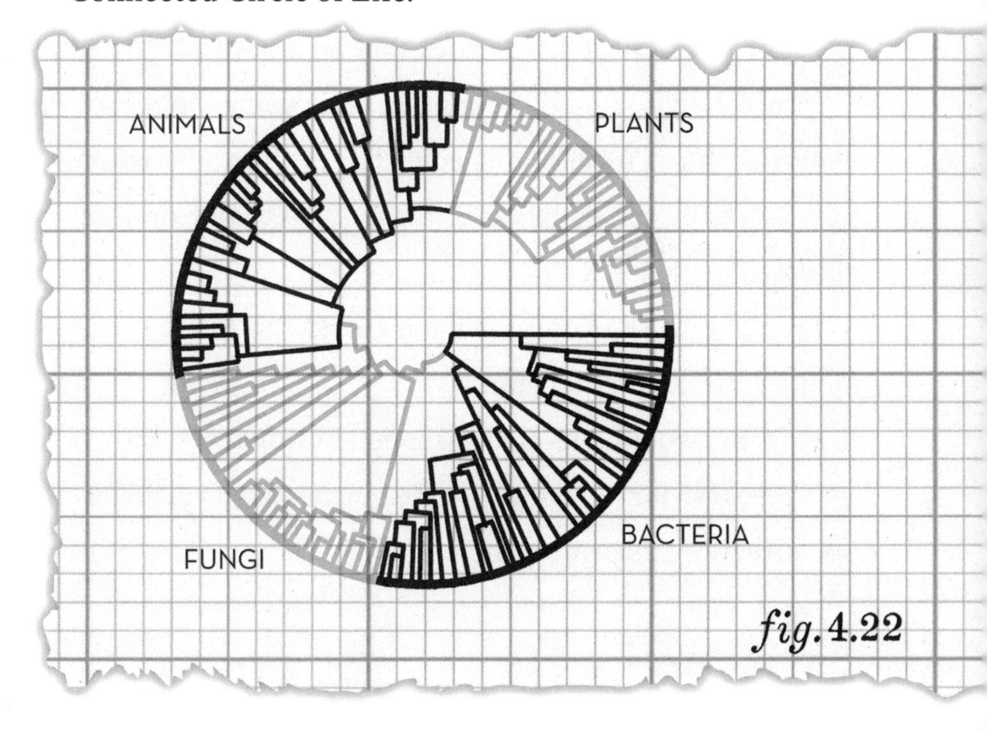

fig. 4.22

Dragonflies (*Ephemera guttulata*) flit in the gold evening light.

Frank turns the Circle of Life compass needle on the EvoBlaster Belt.

"So even at hyperspeed, it would take forever to go backward, then forward to switch species. It makes more sense to jump from spot to spot on the Circle of Life."

Watson laughs, thinking Frank is joking. "Oh yeah. That makes *so much* more sense."

Frank buckles the EvoBlaster Belt on his waist.

"It's like switching TV channels. But using DNA. You evolution-blast from one species to another. The tricky part is setting the compass to blast *back* to your original channel."

Frank spins the compass from *Homo sapiens* to *Buteo jamaicensis*, and back again.

He taps two double-arrow-shaped buttons.

"These fast-forward and reverse buttons send you in just one direction. For emergencies only."

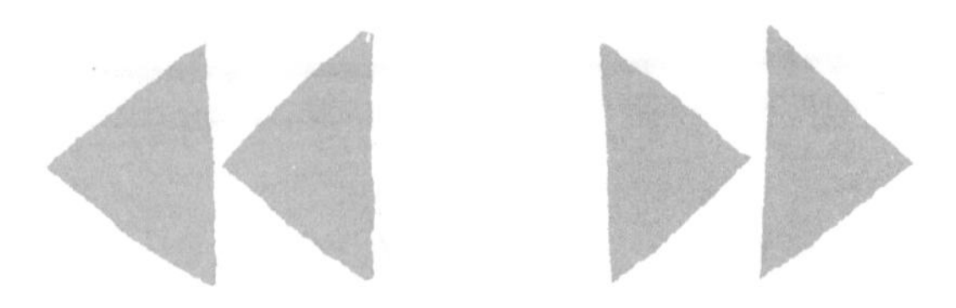

“Oh yeah, of course,” says Watson, still laughing. “Like you could program yourself to change into the Bird Channel and back.”

Frank grins. “Exactly! Now you’ve got it.”

Watson doesn’t get it.

Frank punches the **EVO-PLAY** button on the EvoBlaster Belt.

The belt hums, the gold Circle of Life disk rotates, the compass spins. Frank Einstein’s DNA splits and reforms at hyperspeed. The human shape of Frank shimmers and wavers and suddenly pops into sharp focus as . . .

Bam!

. . . a full-grown *Buteo jamaicensis* (red-tailed hawk).

The magnificent bird leaps into the air, flaps its four-foot wings, and quickly spirals up above the trees.

Klink monitors the data from the EvoBlaster Belt and hums a robot smile.

Klank claps his hands with enthusiastic loud metal crashes.

Watson, stunned, looks up. He calls to the circling hawk, “Frank? Frank?”

“Screeeeeeeee!” answers *Buteo jamaicensis einstein*, “Screeeeeeee!”

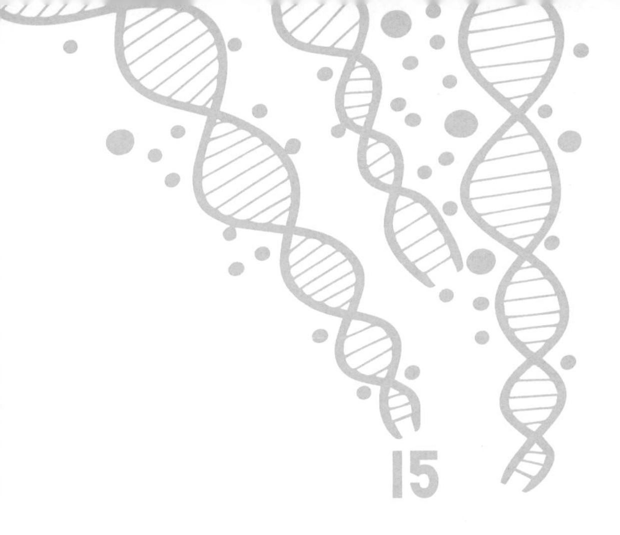

15

E*EEEEEEEEEEEEEEEEEEEEEEE!*" SCREAMS LESLIE.

She runs out of her tent and dives into Janegoodall and Anna's tent.

"I saw his hook! It was reaching into my tent! It was trying to get me!"

Janegoodall and Anna sit up in their sleeping bags.

Janegoodall winks to Anna. Then laughs. "Did the hook look like . . . a wire coat hanger?"

"What? I don't know. Wait a minute . . . Oooooooooo, you guys tricked me."

Leslie and Janegoodall laugh.

"That was scary."

Anna is not laughing. She holds up a coat hanger hook.

"Uh . . . I was going to play that trick on you, but . . . but I didn't get a chance to yet. It wasn't me . . ."

Leslie stops laughing.

"*Eeeeeeeeeeeeeeeeeeeeeeeeeeeee!*"

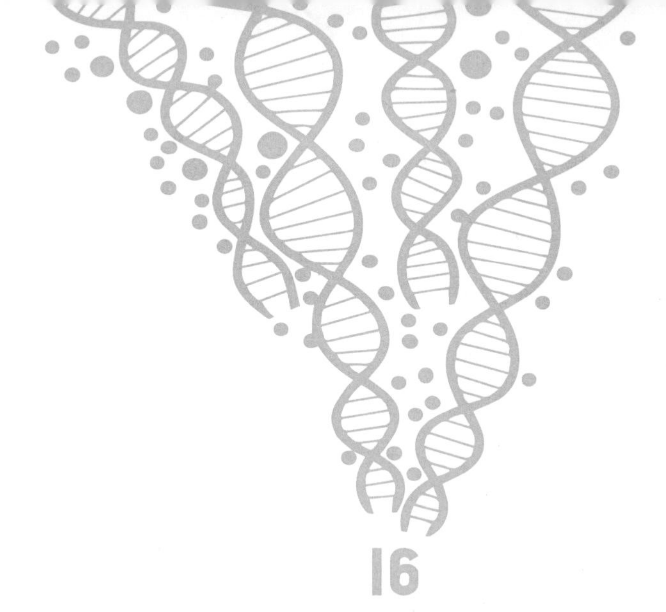

16

B*UTEO JAMAICENSIS EINSTEIN* FLIES DOWN TO EARTH.

The belt reverse beep beep beeps.

The EvoBlaster compass spins back to *Homo sapiens.*

Frank's DNA re-splits and recombines at hyperspeed.

Hawk Frank Einstein devolves, then *evolves.*

Bam!

Frank evo-blasts back to human shape.

"Yes!" cheers Frank. "It works."

"Wow," marvels Watson.

"Now watch this," says Frank.

Homo sapiens Frank sets the EvoBlaster Belt compass again.

Watson looks worried. "Don't you think we should—"

"Nope," says Frank.

He punches the **EVO-PLAY** button.

The EvoBlaster Belt hums, the gold Circle of Life disk rotates, the compass spins.

Frank's DNA splits and reforms at hyperspeed.

Homo sapiens Frank Einstein blurs and evo-blasts into . . . *Tamiasciurus hudsonicus einstein* (American red squirrel Einstein).

Squirrel Frank scrambles up a nearby pine tree.

He is suddenly very hungry for nuts and seeds.

He flips his bushy tail over his head. He digs his sharp claws into the tree bark. He races down the tree trunk and leaps to the ground.

The belt reverse beep beep beeps.

The compass spins.

Bam!

Frank evo-blast-returns to human.

"Man, I would really like a tasty pinecone."

"What if we—" Watson starts to say.

Frank sets the EvoBlaster Belt compass and punches the **EVO-PLAY** button again.

The EvoBlaster Belt hums, the gold Circle of Life disk rotates, the compass spins.

Frank's DNA splits and reforms at hyperspeed.

Homo sapiens Frank Einstein blurs and evo-blasts into . . . *Apis mellifera einstein* (honey bee Einstein).

Honey bee Frank flaps his wings, flying crazy circles around Klank.

He sees Watson split into a hundred Watsons through his compound bee eyes.

He feels, smells, and tastes the forest through his antennae.

He would really like to sink his proboscis into a sweet flower.

The belt reverse beep beep beeps.

The compass spins.

Bam!

Frank scratches his human head.

"I feel like explaining everything in a wiggle dance."

"Well—" begins Watson.

Frank sets the EvoBlaster Belt compass and punches the **EVO-PLAY** button again.

The EvoBlaster Belt hums, the gold Circle of Life disk rotates, the compass spins.

Frank's DNA splits and reforms at hyperspeed.

Homo sapiens Frank Einstein blurs and evo-blasts into . . . *Rubus fruticosus einstein* (blackberry plant Einstein).

Blackberry bush Frank catches sunshine on his leaves.

He pulls in carbon dioxide and releases oxygen.

He probes the soil with his roots.

The belt reverse beep beep beeps.

The compass spins.

Bam!

Human Frank shakes a leg.

"Why do I want to drink a glass of water through my feet?"

Watson raises his hand. "I would like—"

Frank sets the EvoBlaster Belt compass and punches the **EVO-PLAY** button again.

The EvoBlaster Belt hums, the gold Circle of Life disk rotates, the compass spins.

Frank's DNA splits and reforms at hyperspeed.

Homo sapiens Frank Einstein blurs and evo-blasts into . . . *Staphylococcus einstein* (bacteria Einstein).

Bacteria Einstein searches for water.

He searches for nutrition.

He searches for someplace warm.

The belt reverse beep beep beeps.

The compass spins.

Bam!

Human Frank pulls back his arm.

"OK, that was scary. And also, Watson—why is my finger in your nose?"

17

WATSON SHAKES HIS HEAD. "I HAVE NO IDEA. BUT THE EvoBlaster Belt really *can* blast you back and forth into any living shape?"

Frank unbuckles the EvoBlaster Belt and nods. "That was the idea. Just like Grampa Al and Charles Darwin said. It's all connected."

Klink plugs into the belt, and runs a battery of tests.

"Good. Positive. Yes. OK."

Frank checks the position of the setting sun. "OK, so here's our plan. Let's get some sleep. Tomorrow we take the EvoBlaster Belt to Park Area 51. I'll evo-blast into a hawk. Fly over. See what's going on. Then figure out the best life form to use to fix this eco-mess."

Frank casually slings the EvoBlaster Belt over his shoulder.

Watson gives the belt a longing look.

"But . . ."

"Yeah?"

"Well . . . have you ever noticed that every time you make an invention, and we go to sleep, it gets stolen?"

"Yes, that is true," says Klink. "And have you ever noticed that is never *my* fault?" Klink looks at Klank.

Klank looks down and whistles, examining his feet very intently.

"Well, that's not going to happen this time," says Frank. "Because one—nobody but us even *knows* about this invention. Two—T. Edison and Mr. Chimp are nowhere around. And three—we can use Klink's bike lock attachment so the EvoBlaster Belt doesn't get swiped."

Frank turns to head back to camp.

"Yeah, sure. That could work," says Watson. "But before we head back . . . um . . . don't you think it would be . . . uh . . . good scientific method to, you know—test the belt on another life form? Make sure it works on anyone?"

Frank stops and thinks. "That would be good scientific

method. Always good to have someone else duplicate results. But who can we get to do that?"

Klank raises his big metal hand. **"Me! Me! I will evo-blast into . . . an elephant!"**

"Oh, for goodness' sake," says Klink. "Use a few thought cells. You are a robot. Remember?"

"Awwwwwwwwwww," says Klank.

"Klink's right," says Frank. "The EvoBlaster only works on living DNA."

Watson stares at the EvoBlaster Belt and rubs his chin. "You know . . . I could give it a try . . ."

Frank shakes his head. "No, that wouldn't work. Remember you said 'I am not testing any part of this craziness'?"

"Correct," says Klink. "That is exactly what you said. Would you like me to replay a recording of your voice?"

Watson smacks Klink on the side of his glass head. "Well yeah, I did say that. But for the sake of science, you know. And to figure out what's in that creepy Park Area 51. And for the good of the world. I really should help."

"And you would really like to see what it's like to be . . . a cat?"

Watson smiles. "Yes."

Frank looks serious for a second. He taps one finger on his lip. He looks at the belt. He looks at Watson. And then he cracks up laughing. "Heck yeah! Let's get you evo-blasting!"

Frank and Watson, and even non-DNA Klink and Klank, are so excited buckling the belt on Watson and setting the compass to *Felis catus* . . . that they don't even notice another member of the hominid family carefully positioning himself in the tree directly above them.

"You know what, Watson. This is actually a very good idea," says Frank. "Cats have great hearing, even better night vision, and an amazing sense of smell. This might be the perfect form to solve our eco-mystery."

Watson nods.

Frank punches the **EVO-PLAY** button.

The belt hums. The compass spins around the Circle of Life.

And that's when everything goes wrong.

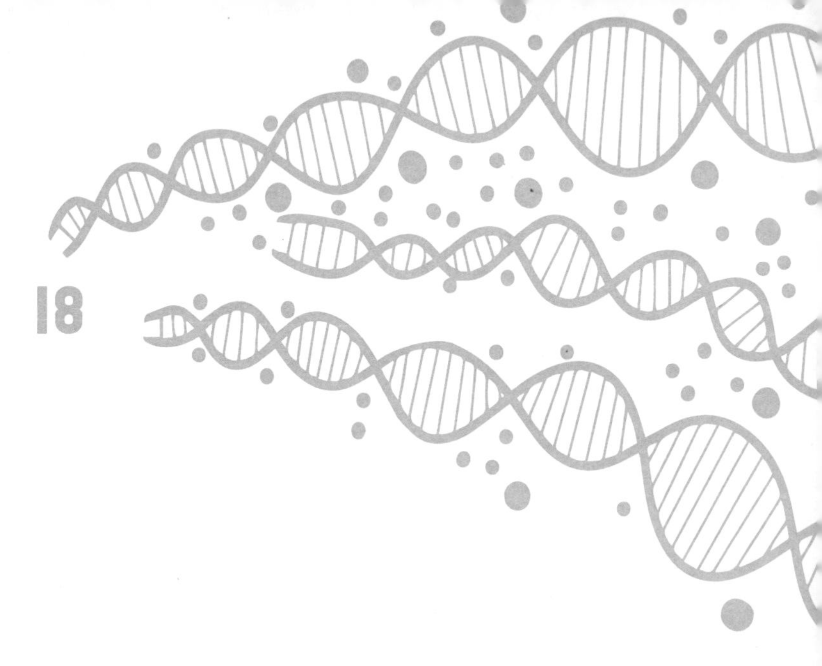

18

A BLAZING ORANGE-RED SUN SETS SLOWLY BEHIND THE LUSH GREEN tree–covered hills of Darwin Park. Forked-tail, curve-winged barn swallows (*Hirundo rustica*) dart in the darkening blue sky overhead. Squirrels climb. Bugs fly. Fish swim in the crystal-clear water of the Darwin River splashing over bluestone rocks and through gullies.

The shadows of coming night cover the stream twisting and turning, plunging under a towering metal wall and . . . suddenly disappearing into a long, low, black steel building where . . .

T. Edison stands on a metal mesh platform overlooking a crashing, clanking, hissing, whooshing, rumbling factory line.

"*Why?!*" yells T. Edison, smacking a big green **SPEED** button on the master control panel.

"Why do I *always* have to do *everything*?!"

The hissing and whooshing and rumbling of the bottling line speeds up.

"I fill the bottle-blowing machine!"

T. Edison smacks the handrail.

Smack!

"I feed the washing and capping machine!!"

Smack!

"I tune the labeling and shrink-wrapping machine!!!"

Smack!

"That stupid monkey doesn't understand anything! He doesn't get it. You have to be the *boss* of Nature! Smack it, bend it to your will!"

T. Edison stomps down the metal-grating steps to the factory floor. He mutters out loud to himself.

"*I* am the genius around here. Why am *I* stuck doing all the work? *I* think up all the great ideas for inventions. *I* make it all possible."

T. Edison ducks inside the line of water bottles snaking around the machinery. He picks a bottle off the line.

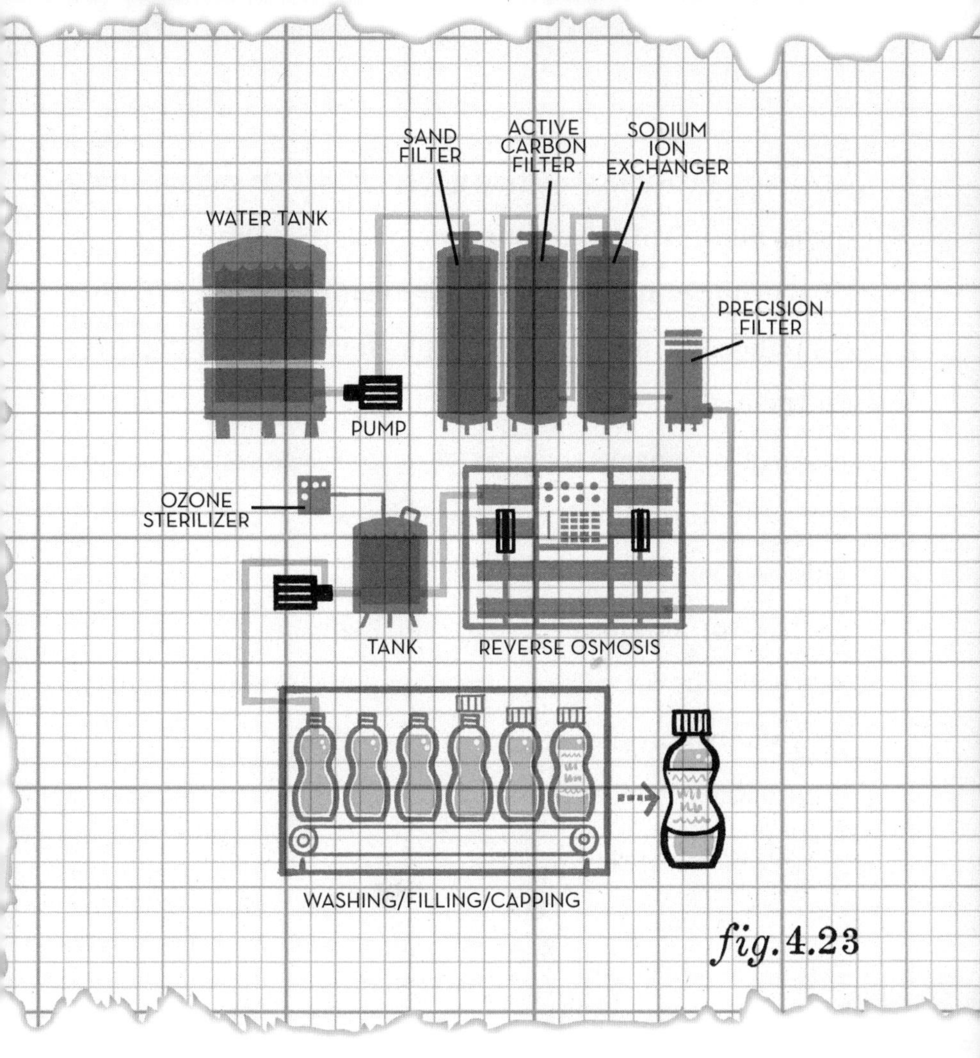

fig. 4.23

He admires its simple label.

Nature Good

"Stupid consumers don't even know they are just buying stream water. I saved a lot of money by not messing around with a water purifier, too."

T. Edison checks his watch.

"Almost bedtime. And that goofy primate is still out messing around. Well, I've got news for that chimp. He is now a part-time employee. No more health benefits. No more insurance. No more library books for him. And I'm done for the night. I'm going to bed!"

T. Edison smacks the red **STOP** button. The water-bottling assembly line rumbles, clanks, hisses to a stop. And it is suddenly very quiet. And a little scary.

T. Edison stomps over to a small bedroom with a cot. He puts on his favorite Transformer pajamas and climbs under his Spider-Man sheets.

Outside, a cricket chirps.

Water drips.

T. Edison takes out his phone and dials the one number saved in it.

"Hello, sweetie!"

"Hello, Mother."

"Are you and Mr. Chimpy Whimpy having fun on your camping trip?"

T. Edison turns sideways on his Spider-Man pillow. "Yes, production—I mean camping is good."

"That's nice."

"I just called to—you know . . . say good night."

"Of course, sweetie," says Mrs. Edison. She sing-songs, "Good night."

T. Edison answers, "Sleep tight."

They both finish, "Don't let the bedbugs bite."

T. Edison hangs up. He smiles. He gets out of bed and smacks the green **START** button. The assembly line jumps into rattling production again.

T. Edison lies back in bed, listening to the hum and crash of free water being turned into bottled money.

He crosses his hands behind his head and smiles.

T. Edison loves to be the boss.

Of absolutely everything.

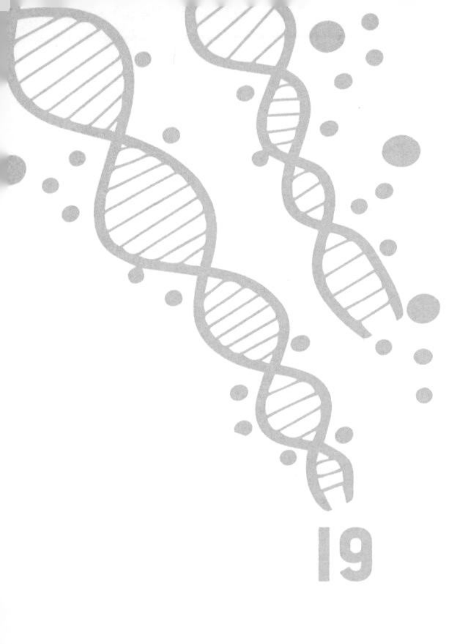

19

THE EVOBLASTER BELT HUMS AND BEGINS HYPERSPEED SPLITTING and recombining Watson's DNA.

Mr. Chimp activates the almost-invisible trigger wire he has rigged to a huge dead tree.

Deeper in the woods, the rigged tree leans, spins, and falls with a forest-shaking *crrrraaaash!*

Klink, Klank, and Frank jump.

They turn back to look for the cause of the noisy crash.

And in that five seconds of distraction, Mr. Chimp drops from the tree, grabs the EvoBlaster Belt, and swings back up to his hiding place in the heavily leafed linden tree (*Tilia cordata*)—unseen by anyone except the half-evo-blasted Watson.

"Wow," says Klank. **"That was a big tree."**

"No kidding," says Frank. "We can check that after—"

Frank stops.

He looks at the spot where Watson is supposed to be testing the EvoBlaster Belt.

Watson has evo-blasted into a house cat (*Felis catus watson*).

But something is missing.

"Hey," says Klank. **"Where is the belt?"**

"Calculating possible malfunctions now," says Klink.

Frank and Klank look all around the meadow, in the woods, across the pond.

No belt.

"EvoBelt systems all fine," reports Klink. "There's a 99.9 percent possibility that belt was removed just as Watson evo-blasted into the form of this *Felis catus*."

Frank raises his eyebrows. "Oh boy."

"Meow?" asks *Felis catus watson.*

Frank kneels down, picks up the gray tabby cat, and pets it. "Don't worry, Watson. Everything's fine. You will be back to human in three minutes. Just as long as the **POWER** button on the belt doesn't get turned off. Because that, um . . . erases your return to *Homo sapiens* code . . ."

"Meow," says *Felis catus watson,* looking up into the tree above them. *"Meow!"*

A leathery finger presses the **POWER** button on the belt.

The spinning compass slows to a stop.

The EvoBlaster's lights dim, and it powers off.

Mr. Chimp swings away.

Felis catus watson jumps from Frank's arms and claws up the tree, madly chasing the disappearing shape—his one, and only, hope to return to human form.

CHAMP

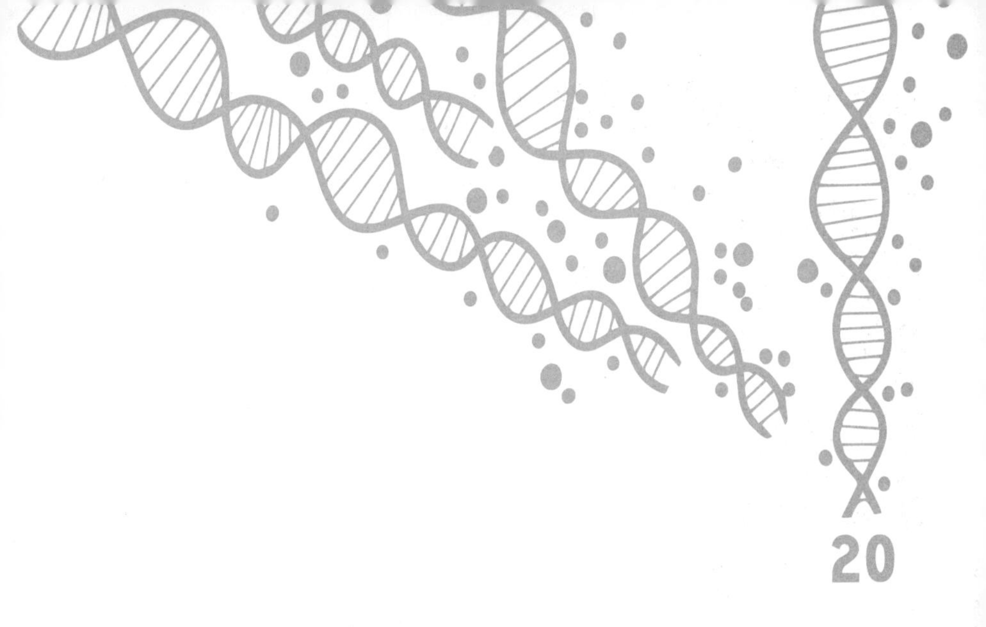

20

HIGH IN AN AMERICAN HORNBEAM TREE (*CARPINUS CAROLINIANA*).

Mr. Chimp puts the finishing touches on his night nest. He weaves one last leafy branch into the snugly padded bowl of sticks and leaves, settles in, and leans back against the smooth gray trunk.

He looks around. That pesky cat is long lost, and nowhere to be seen.

Mr. Chimp places his ladybug backpack gently between his rough feet.

Field crickets (*Gryllus assimilis*) chirp their evening call.

Mr. Chimp takes off his **SECURITY** hat and places it gently on the edge of his nest.

Spring peepers (*Pseudacris crucifer*) peep, calling for mates.

Mr. Chimp opens his pack and unconsciously holds his breath as he pulls out his prize.

The bright full moon shines through the hornbeam branches and lights up—a belt. A large, wired gold belt with a compass dial.

The chorus of crickets and katydids and peepers trills in the clear night air.

Mr. Chimp examines the belt controls. He thinks he probably should bring the belt to T. Edison. They can test it. Imitate it. Make it *their* invention.

But . . .

Maybe not.

What has T. Edison done with all Mr. Chimp's good ideas? Except mess them up?

Mr. Chimp stands up in his nest.

Mr. Chimp buckles the EvoBlaster belt on his waist. It feels good.

The crickets chirp a beat slower as the night air cools.

Mr. Chimp has watched every PBS special about apes (and monkeys) and evolution. Twice.

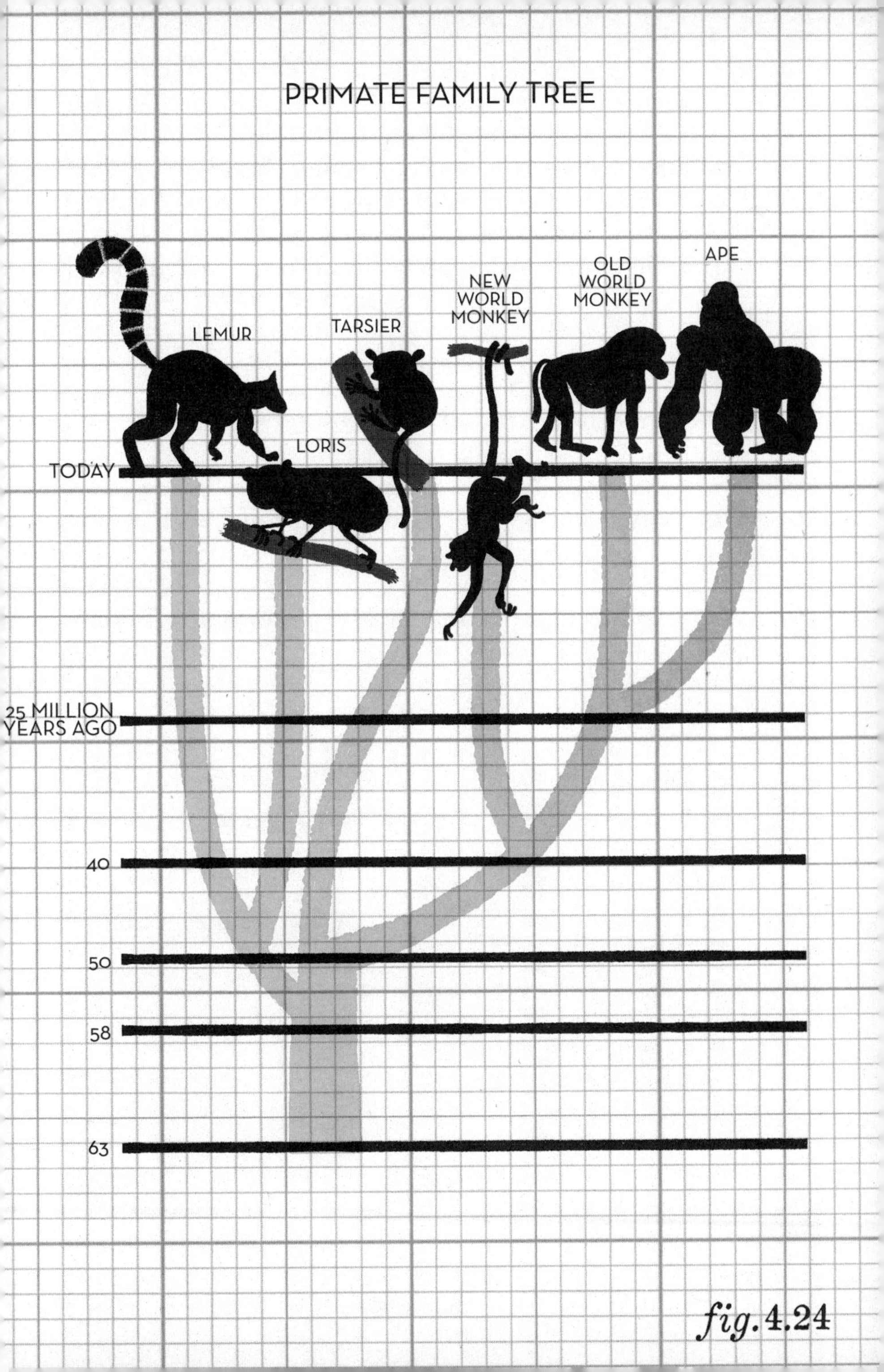
PRIMATE FAMILY TREE
LEMUR
TARSIER
NEW WORLD MONKEY
OLD WORLD MONKEY
APE
LORIS
TODAY
25 MILLION YEARS AGO
40
50
58
63

fig. 4.24

He knows more about the primate family tree than T. Edison ever will.

Mr. Chimp idly taps the **REVERSE** button on the EvoBlaster belt.

He knows that he and T. Edison came from a common ancestor who lived around eight million years ago.

The peepers peep louder, competing to sing the loudest.

Mr. Chimp knows that 98.8 percent of his DNA and T. Edison's DNA is the same.

And that he has an extra pair of chromosomes. Twenty-four to T. Edison's twenty-three.

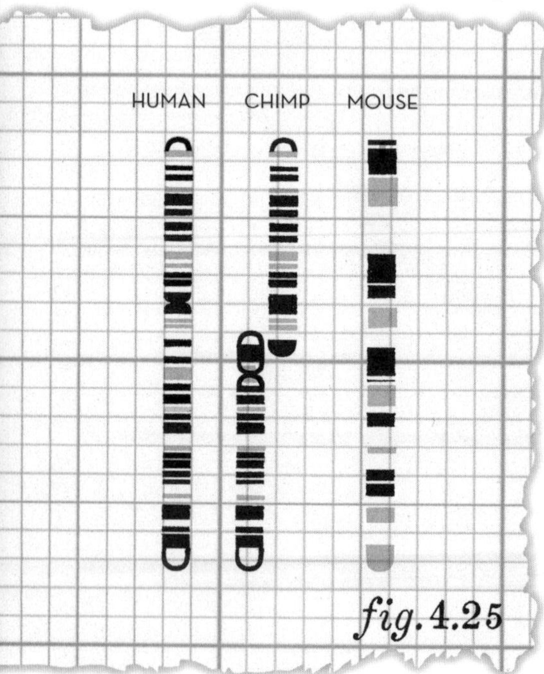

fig. 4.25

Mr. Chimp taps the **FAST-FORWARD** button on the EvoBlaster Belt.

What he doesn't know is what no one knows . . .

A warm night wind sways Mr. Chimp's nesting tree. Silver moonbeams light the woods in spooky effect. The chorus of calling peepers, crickets, and katydids swells in a screaming crescendo.

. . . what might a chimpanzee (*Pan troglodytes*) evolve into in the far future?

The full moon slips behind a cloud.

It is too dark to see exactly which button is pressed by Mr. Chimp's leathery index finger.

But a hum, a glow, the whir of a spinning golden circle, then *pooooom!* A flash of yellow lights up the night woods, scaring every insect, bird, and animal in the woods silent.

The wind blows.

Clouds glide overhead.

The reappearing moon lights up something standing in Mr. Chimp's sleeping nest.

Something not chimpanzee.

Something not human.

Something not ever seen before in this world.

A Future-Evolved Super Chimp.

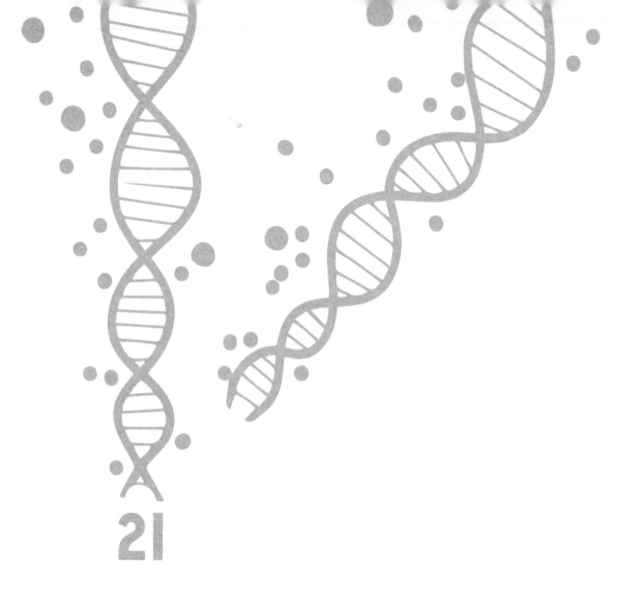

21

FRANK POWERS OFF THE CAMP LIGHT, SNUGGLES DOWN IN HIS sleeping bag, and quickly falls asleep.

Outside Frank's tent, Klank sits on the ground, awkwardly squeezing the gray tabby cat in a flexi-arm hug. **"But what are we going to do?"**

Klink parks himself by the camp workbench. "Like Frank Einstein said: There is nothing we can do to-night. So power down. Save your energy. Tomorrow morning we get inside Area 51."

Klank hugs the cat tighter. **"But oh, poor Watson!"**

"Mrrrroww!" gasps the squashed cat.

Klink powers down.

Klank tries to pet the cat, but mostly just bonks its head with his robot fingers.

"Don't worry, Watson. Frank Einstein has a plan to get you back."

"Meoooowww meow meow meow," answers *Felis catus watson.*

"Whoooooo," hoots the great horned owl across the field. *"Whoo whoo."*

• • •

Janegoodall rechecks all her supplies in her backpack. She powers off the camp light, and snuggles down in her sleeping bag.

Leslie sits up, still wide-eyed. “But what are we going to do?”

Anna folds her arms behind her head. “Like Janegoodall said: There is nothing we can do tonight. So save your energy. Tomorrow morning we will cover the area, and investigate that Area 51.”

Leslie hugs her knees tighter. “I didn’t sign up for scary science. Who would be trying to scare us?”

“*Whoooooo,*” hoots the great horned owl across the field. “*Whoo whoo.*”

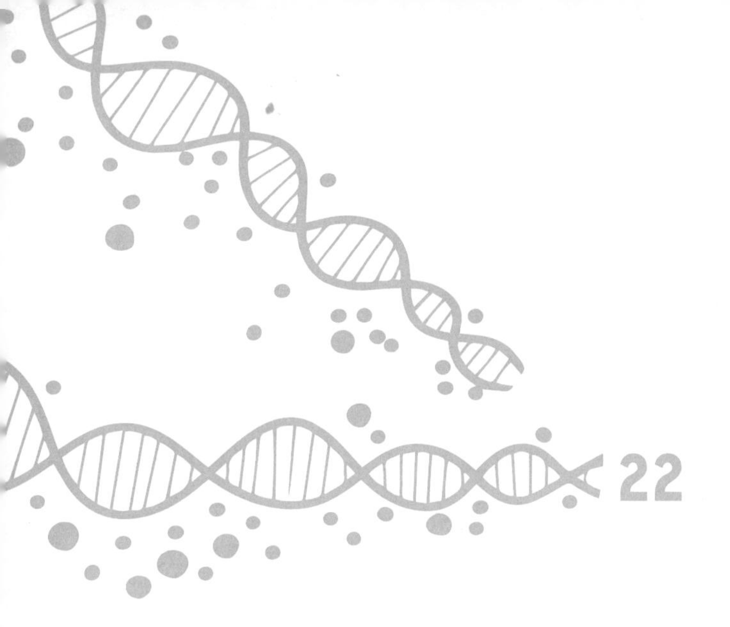

22

MORNING DAWNS. SOFT SUNLIGHT DAPPLES THE Nature Good factory picnic yard in the heart of Darwin Park. Mourning doves (*Zenaida macroura*) coo. Pine trees (*Pinus strobus*) sway in the gentle breeze.

Chickens (*Gallus gallus domesticus*) wander the yard.

T. Edison notices none of this.

Because he is sitting at the breakfast picnic table, staring at the invention in his hands, given to him by Mr. Chimp, which is almost too amazing to believe.

"Wow! You mean this thing can really blast someone around evolution?"

Mr. Chimp holds up the book he is reading and nods a truthful *yes*.

T. Edison taps the double-arrow-shaped buttons on the EvoBlaster Belt.

"So I can evolve into a smarter future me by going **REVERSE**, then **FAST-FORWARD**?"

Mr. Chimp finishes his breakfast bowl of Ant Granola and nods a lying *yes*.

T. Edison examines the belt.

"Amazing. And very fine work bringing this to me, Mr. Chimp. Why, I was saying to myself just last night what a wonderful VP and CFO you are."

Mr. Chimp, not believing a word of it, signs:

T. Edison buckles the belt around his waist. He poses like he just won something.

"We should test this out."

Mr. Chimp nods a very encouraging *yes*. His plan to trick Edison, and get rid of him, is falling right into place.

T. Edison struts around the yard. "Of course I completely understand how this works. I *am* a genius, you know."

Mr. Chimp signs:

Mr. Chimp wanders over to push the **REVERSE** button, devolve Edison back into a fish . . . or maybe farther . . . an amoeba!

Then Mr. Chimp will be free to evolve himself into a Future Chimp, take over Edison Industries, and run the world all on his own.

With T. Edison in a glass bowl on Mr. Chimp's desk.

"I'm just saying we should test it out to make sure that numbskull Einstein didn't hook it up wrong."

T. Edison struts around the yard, showing off the belt. He flexes his arms. Awkwardly. He puffs out his chest. Weakly. He throws a fake punch at a flower. He karate kicks a rock.

"Owww! Owww! Owww!"

T. Edison punches the flower off its stem, then raises his hands overhead and announces himself, "Teeeeeeeeeee Edisoooooooooon! Champion of the Worrrrrlllllllld!"

T. Edison rubs a finger over the double-arrow buttons.

Mr. Chimp signs:

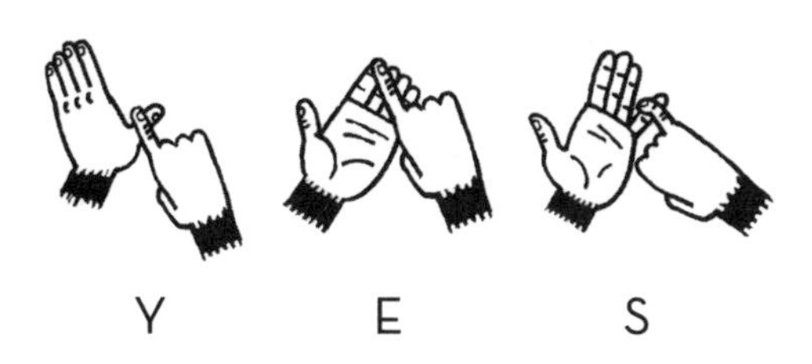

Mr. Chimp can feel the whole world bowing to him.

T. Edison pauses.

"Yes! You are right, Mr. Chimp. Yes!" T. Edison takes off the EvoBlaster Belt and holds it out to Mr. Chimp. "And *you* should be the one to test it!"

Mr. Chimp tries not to look panicked. This was not the plan. He needs to devolve Edison first.

Mr. Chimp tries to think of a good excuse.

Mr. Chimp rubs his stomach and makes a frowning face.

"You have a stomachache? Oh, you are such a chicken!" Edison kicks another rock. A very small one this time. "Chicken, chicken . . . *bawwwk bawwk bawwwk . . .*" Edison teases Mr. Chimp.

Mr. Chimp tries to think of another plan to trick

T. Edison into punching the **REVERSE** button himself. He goes back to reading.

There is grandeur in this view of life . . . from so simple a beginning endless forms most beautiful and most wonderful have been, and are being, evolved.

The real chickens wandering around the factory yard hear T. Edison and answer him, *"Bawwwwk bawwwk bawwwk."*

One of the baby chicks, curious, hops inside the ring made by the belt.

"Aha!" says Edison. "Well, here's a genius idea—if you are too chicken to test this, Mr. Chimp, I will have a *real* chicken try it."

Mr. Chimp puts a finger inside his book to save his place and looks up.

Mr. Chimp knows what birds evolved from. He knows this is not a good idea.

Mr. Chimp raises his hand to sign and explain.

But he's too late.

T. Edison pushes the **REVERSE** button. With the baby chick inside the EvoBlaster Belt.

The Belt hums. The compass spins backward. The

electromagnetic field formed inside the belt reverses, unraveling and disconnecting the chicken's DNA molecules, emergency reverse devolving the chicken to what its ancestors *were*.

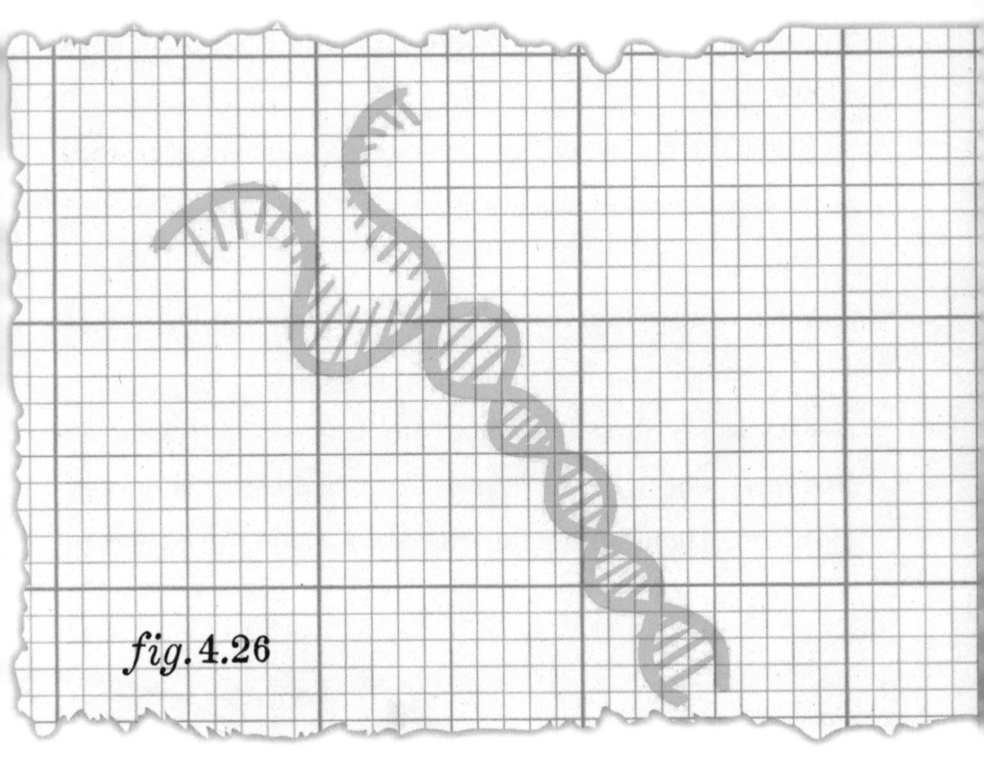

fig. 4.26

The chicken shimmers and gives a very un-chickenlike sound. *"EEeeeeewwwaawwwk!"*

T. Edison watches, actually hopping in excitement.

Mr. Chimp puts his book down, and slowly backs away.

The EvoBlaster Belt hums louder.

The compass spins faster.

Evolution reverses. At hyperspeed.

The chicken shape inside the belt stretches out, grows up, drops feathers, sprouts teeth, hardens scales, thickens claws . . .

The baby chick swiftly devolves to what its ancestors were seventy million years ago.

Bam!

What used to be a baby chick shakes the EvoBlaster Belt off one scaled and fearsomely clawed foot.

Mr. Chimp does not waste any time signing what he feared . . . and what he knows is the name of this hungry carnivore. He jumps up into the nearest tree and swings to

safety, away from one of the most fearsome superpredators of all time.

"BAWWWWWWWKKKGGGGRRRRRR!" roars the baby (but still gigantic) and very scary-looking T. rex.

"Oh . . . my . . . goodness," squeaks T. Edison.

Which is a mistake.

Because the squeak attracts the attention of the T. rex.

And T. rex turns its hungry-predator eye on one suddenly chicken T. Edison.

DO NOT
ENTER
Nature Good

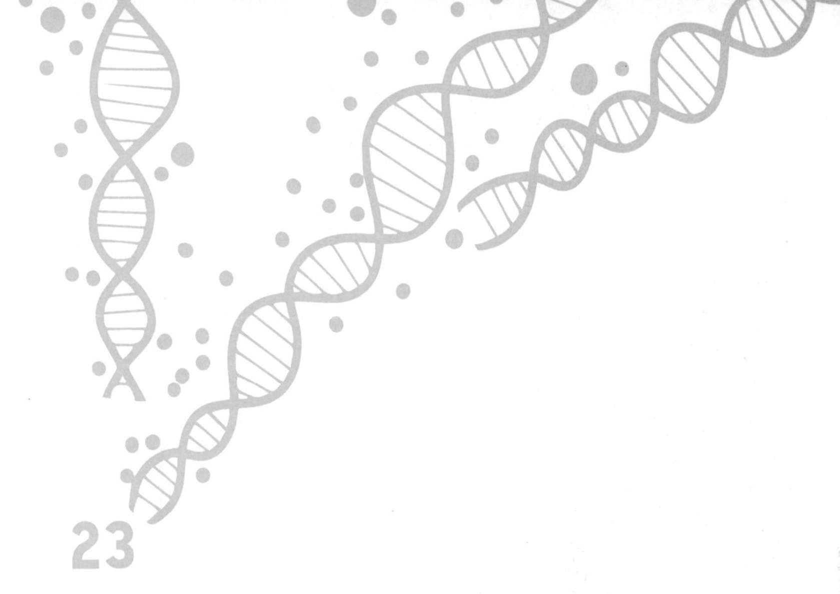

23

MORNING DAWNS. SOFT SUNLIGHT DAPPLES THE FOREST floor in the heart of Darwin Park. Mourning doves (*Zenaida macroura*) coo. Pine trees (*Pinus strobus*) sway in the gentle breeze.

Frank Einstein, Klink, and Klank stand at the base of a very tall black woven-metal fence with a huge sign:

DO NOT ENTER

Nature Good

The gray tabby cat in Frank's arms looks up at the top of the wall and explains, *"Meow. Meow meow, meow meow meow."*

"OK," answers Frank. "Don't panic, Watson. I have a plan."

Franks feels terrible that his invention got his pal into this mess.

"The only way to get you back to human is to get the belt. I'm pretty sure you're trying to tell us it's on the other side of this fence. So we have to get in here."

"Meeeeeeeeow," agrees Watson.

"We can turn into giant elephants and smash down the wall!" says Klank. He takes a running start. He smashes into the metal fence with a *bong!* Klank falls back on the forest floor.

"Great idea," says Klink. "You just forgot to turn into an elephant. Stand back. I may be able to bore a hole with my drill attachment."

Klink extends his drill attachment. It spins at high speed. It smokes and whines.

It doesn't even leave a mark on the mystery metal.

"Meow," says Watson. He jumps on Klink's shoulder.

Frank pets Watson's head. He looks up at the top of the fence. He looks up at the trees leaning over the top of the fence. "I think it's up to you, pal. You are going to have to climb up the tree, get on the other side of the fence, and find the belt so we can get you back to human."

"Meeeeeeeoooowwwwww," says Watson. But this time he looks very panicked.

There is a sudden noise of cracking sticks in the underbrush. The bushes shake. A shadowy hunchbacked figure appears.

"Oh no!" says Klank. **"What is that?! It is a little Bigfoot!"**

"Janegoodall?" says Frank. "What are you doing out here in the woods?"

"Frank Einstein? Klink! Klank!" calls Janegoodall, brushing the burrs off her Science Scout shorts and backpack. "I was going to ask you the same thing."

"We were out here looking into some weird things happening in this ecosystem. We found this place"—Frank smacks the black fence—"and someone has been trying to scare us off."

"No!" says Janegoodall. "Someone has been trying to

scare off my Science Scout troop, too. Anna and Leslie are tracking this fence north. I've taken south. Looking for a way in."

"Meeeeooowww."

"Cute cat," says Janegoodall, petting the gray tabby.

"It is not a cat. It is Watson," says Klank.

"What?" asks Janegoodall.

"Ummmm . . . well . . . ah . . . yes," says Frank. "That is true. See, I invented an EvoBlaster Belt so we could get inside this Park Area 51. The Belt lets you hyperquickly evolve forward or backward . . . into any species."

"You are kidding."

"Frank Einstein is not kidding," reports Klink.

"But something snatched the belt while Watson was making an evo-blast . . . and he got stuck . . . uh . . . as this cat."

Watson flattens his ears. "GRrrrrrrrrrr."

Janegoodall stops petting *Felis catus watson*. "Sorry, Watson."

"So now we really have to get in there to get my invention back . . ."

"GRrrrrrrr."

". . . and return Watson to human."

"How can I help?" asks Janegoodall.

The morning quiet is broken by a faint roar of a noise from inside Area 51.

Felis catus watson looks up.

Frank Einstein and Janegoodall look up.

"What in the world was that?"

"My instruments have detected something," says Klink. "But it is something that should not exist."

24

"BAWWWWWKKKKKKRRRRRRR!"

What used to be a baby chicken, now a twenty-foot-tall baby T. rex, cocks its massive head sideways. It chomps its flesh-ripping teeth. It twitches its long green scaly and feathered tail, smashing a good-sized tree in the Edison factory yard to splinters.

"Yeeeeek!" T. Edison gasps again.

The T. rex takes a step toward T. Edison.

"Niiiiice chicken dinosaur . . . Gooood chicken dinosaur . . ." T. Edison half-sings, half-says. He backs slowly toward the safety of the steel factory door, holding his bag of Cheezy Puffs out in front of him.

The T. rex wiggles its short, two-clawed front limbs. It rakes the ground with its massive three-toed foot claws.

T. Edison takes another step back. "What a friendly chicken dinosaur . . ."

The T. rex snaps its toothy jaws. It does not look at all friendly. It looks mad. And hungry.

T. Edison throws a Cheezy Puff on the ground in front of it.

The T. rex pauses, licks up the Cheezy Puff.

Without taking

his eye off the dinosaur, T. Edison calls to Mr. Chimp, sitting safely in a tree. "Oh, Mr. Chimp? This might be a good time to gather the chickens. *This one* especially."

Mr. Chimp sits back in his safe tree perch. He considers this latest development. This may be an *easier* way to get rid of T. Edison.

Mr. Chimp answers T. Edison with a noncommittal *"Ooook."*

"BAWWWWWKKKKKKKRRRRR!"

The T. rex suddenly hop-jumps a step closer to T. Edison.

"Shhoooooo! Bad chicken dinosaur! Go away, chicken dinosaur!"

Mr. Chimp, sitting back, dangles a foot off his tree branch.

T. Edison backs toward the factory door. But he knows he is still too far away to beat even a chicken, let alone a T. rex, in a race.

"You know what I have been thinking, Mr. Chimp? That you should be an equal vice president in our great Nature Good water business—"

T. Edison throws a last handful of Cheezy Puffs at the T. rex's scaly, clawed feet.

"BAWWWWWKKKKKKKRRRRR!"

The T. rex stomps the Cheezy Puffs to orange dust. It crouches, getting ready to jump on a much better, warm-blooded *Homo sapiens* meal.

"I mean *president* of the business!" T. Edison shuffles back as fast as he can.

Mr. Chimp thinks about being president.

He decides he will save T. Edison.

For now.

"Ooooooook," agrees Mr. Chimp.

Mr. Chimp goes crazy shaking the tree branches with both feet and both hands. He jumps up and down. He distracts the T. rex, hooting, *"Eeee eee Ahhh Ahh Oooo Oooo!"*

The startled T. rex stops, and looks up.

T. Edison sprints for the factory door.

The T. rex looks back, spots its dinner slipping away. It charges.

T. Edison fumbles with the handle. Swings the door open. Dives inside as the T. rex lunges, jaws wide open.

Whammmmm! The T. rex slams right into the steel door, knocking it shut—sending T. Edison flying inside to land on the factory floor.

T. Edison, terrified, dazed, but safe . . . sits up.

"Good heavens! A chicken devolved into a T. rex? What could be worse?"

Outside, from up in the tree, **Nature Good** president Chimp watches the baby T. rex prowling the yard.

"Bawwwwwwkkkkrrrrr!"

The dinosaur claws at the dirt, accidentally knocking one of the North American black ants (*Camponotus pennsylvanicus*) from Mr. Chimp's breakfast, and it lands inside the EvoBlaster Belt.

Then the T. rex turns away, slapping its dino tail against the EvoBlaster Belt **FAST-FORWARD** button.

The belt hums, the gold wheel spins forward, the ant shimmers, DNA recombines, and—*Bam!*—superspeed fast-forward evolves . . .

President Chimp sees, in living 3-D, exactly what could be worse than a chicken devolved into a T. rex.

T. Edison takes a peek, then slams the factory door and locks himself in his Edison Safe Room.

"Ooooh ooook," breathes Mr. Chimp.

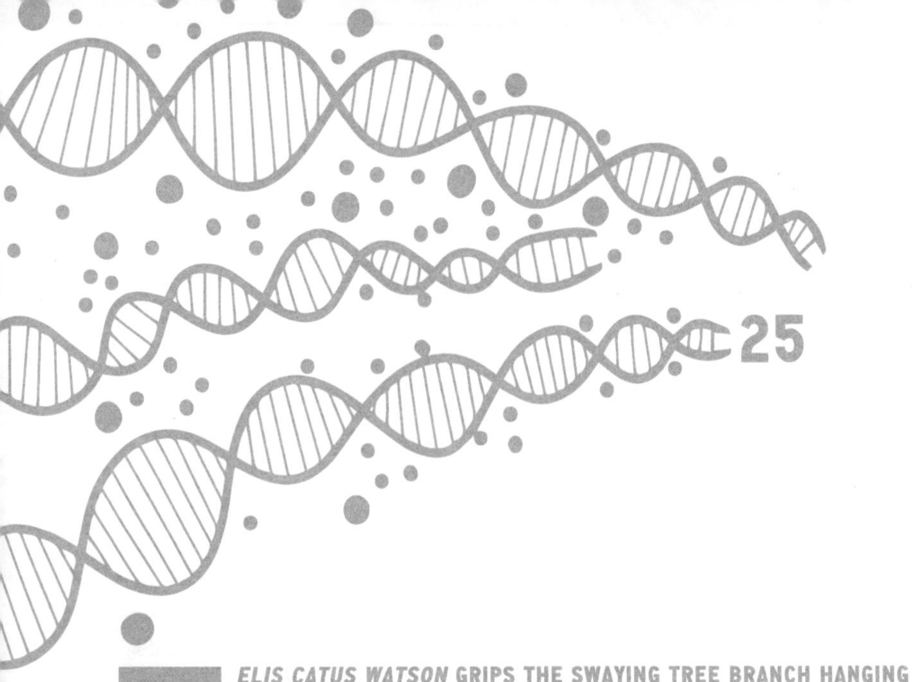

25

FELIS CATUS WATSON GRIPS THE SWAYING TREE BRANCH HANGING over the towering metal fence, terrified, claws on all four paws dug in.

"You can do it!" Frank Einstein calls from far below.

Cat Watson looks down, then out across the hidden woods.

He is not so sure he can do it.

But then Cat Watson hears noises. Sounds too faint, too high-pitched for human ears.

Cat Watson sees movement deep in the woods. Details in the shadows too faint for human eyes.

Cat Watson lifts his head. He twitches his whiskers. In the morning breeze his extrasensitive cat nose smells:

a sharp acid insect tang

a musky lizard funk

a pungent ape fur odor

a weird metallic cheese whiff

and . . . and . . . maybe . . . a faint scent of plastic/human/ metal wiring.

Cat Watson rises high on the swaying branch, all senses now alert, muscles tense, suddenly full-predator fearless.

Cat Watson leaps from his branch, over the wall, tree to tree, down to pine needle–soft ground. He runs, leaps, follows his cat senses to the commotion of sights and sounds and smells ahead. He ducks under the bush at the edge of the clearing. Peeks out. And stops. Stunned.

Cat Watson wonders if there is something wrong with his cat eyes.

Not because of the giant black pipe sucking water out of the Darwin River into the low gray factory building.

But maybe because of the real live green-scaled

and spotty-feathered *Tyrannosaurus rex* smashing the factory picnic table.

And definitely because of the twenty-foot-long black *ANT* angrily waving its ten-foot antennae in front of the T. rex.

Cat Watson shakes his cat head.

"BAWWWWWWWKKKKKK!" roars the T. rex.

"CHCHCHCHCHCHCHCH!" the monster ANT answers the challenge.

Nope. These creatures are real. And the fight is on.

The ANT jumps. It snaps its massive armored jaws around a T. rex leg.

The T. rex screams . . . and bites off one of the ANT's six telephone-pole-sized legs with a *crack!*

The giant ANT lifts the T. rex completely off the ground. And smashes it back down with a truly earthshaking *WHAMMMMM!*

The monster ANT and T. rex thrash and flop and crash through trees, down the hill, into the black pipe—breaking it. A gushing column of water explodes, rushing back into its original streambed.

Cat Watson spots T. Edison—running for the back of the

half-wrecked factory. Up above, a noise—Mr. Chimp in the branch of a tree.

Exactly, thinks Watson. *Exactly who I thought was behind this mess. But where where where is the—*

Mr. Chimp looks down.

Watson looks to where Mr. Chimp is looking.

On the ground, under the splintered picnic table.

There!

The EvoBlaster Belt!

The T. rex and towering ANT thrash and scream and roar and fight.

Cat Watson doesn't think twice. He doesn't think at all. He acts on pure powerful animal instinct.

Cat Watson jumps from the bush. He dodges left and right and under the legs of the battling dinosaur and ant. He races directly below a surprised Mr. Chimp, bites the belt between sharp feline teeth, and runs.

"Nooooooooooo!" cries T. Edison, watching the unpiped river wash the rest of his factory downstream.

"Ooooooookkkk!" yells Mr. Chimp, seeing his dream of the future disappearing in a cat's jaws.

"BAWWWWWWWKK!" screams the T. rex, spotting a better dinner than the ANT.

"CHCHCHCHCHCHCH!" chitters the ANT, still looking to fight.

Cat Watson leaps and hops and runs for the wall.

With one desperate ape, one hungry dinosaur, and one very large and very mad ANT chasing close behind.

26

FRANK EINSTEIN AND JANEGOODALL PACE BACK AND FORTH AT THE base of the fence.

The sun rises higher in the sky.

"Watson's been gone for a very long time," says Janegoodall.

Frank bites his thumb. "I should have come up with a better plan. If he gets stuck being a cat, it's going to be really hard to explain to his mom."

A flock of crows (*Corvus brachyrhynchos*) caws excitedly on the other side of the fence.

A whoosh and a thump. Something hits the fence.

"Water!" says Klank. **"The river is back!"**

And sure enough—under the fence, the dry streambed of the Darwin River slowly refills.

Thump, crash, caw sounds come from behind the fence. Trees cracking, roaring, insect clicking.

Klink checks his seismograph attachment. "I am calculating the same conclusion as before. But these results cannot be right."

Everyone looks up, just as a cat lands lightly atop the fence. A cat holding in its mouth a slightly altered championship-wrestling belt.

Frank cheers, "Watson! You did it!"

Smash thump boom. Something hits the fence again. Water spurts like a small geyser now.

"Drop the belt! I'll spin it to get you back to human."

Crash! The fence tilts, creaks, leans.

Cat Watson drops the belt.

A dark shape swings on a vine, swoops, grabs the falling belt, and lands on top of the fence.

"Good heavens!" gasps Janegoodall.

"Mr. Chimp!" curses Frank.

And *BLAAAAMMMMM!* The fence collapses.

The torrent of water pushing the fence gushes into the streambed.

Cat Watson leaps for the nearest tree.

Mr. Chimp, still clutching the belt, falls.

A giant scaly, clawed foot kicks down a whole section of fence.

A colossal-sized ANT stomps over the fallen fence piece, and scans the area with its feelers.

"What in the world—?" says Janegoodall, not believing what she is seeing.

Mr. Chimp lands with a thump and loses his grip on the belt. He crawls to grab it, but sees a sharp-toothed dinosaur on one side, and an impossibly large ant on the other.

Mr. Chimp, no fool, jumps up and runs leaps swings for safety as fast as he can.

"Holy evolution!" gasps Frank Einstein, crouched behind a log. "Talk about All Interconnected Life. This is amazing."

Two towering figures step forward.

"This is such great proof. From microscopic bugs . . . to the biggest beasts. We all evolved. We are *all* connected."

Up in the tree, Watson nods. He is not thinking this is so amazing. He is thinking this is crazy. He is thinking this is scary.

He would say something. But he can't.

And he really would like to, because he is seriously worried that this time Frank Einstein will not be able to think his way out of a jam.

"Don't worry, Watson," says Frank. "I'll think of something."

"BBBAAWWWKKKKRRR!" growls the megapredator.

"CHHHHKKKKCHHHKKKK!" rattles the monster next to it.

Both slowly turn and look at the humans crouched behind the log.

"Uh-oh" says Frank Einstein, suddenly realizing what it feels like to not be kings of the food chain. "It's survival of the *smartest* now."

The hungry T. rex and monster ANT advance on their new prey.

Frank Einstein quickly figures what has happened. Someone has misused the **FAST-FORWARD** and **REVERSE** buttons.

Frank Einstein calculates. Frank Einstein pieces together a new plan.

"Janegoodall, do you have anything sweet we can use to distract the ant?"

"Right," says Janegoodall, digging in her backpack. "Because ants communicate with smells." She pulls out her chocolate energy bars.

"Great."

Frank calls to Klank and Klink.

"Klank! Tease the dinosaur and draw him toward you! Janegoodall and I will distract the ANT over this way! Then, Klink, you race in and grab the belt!"

Klank lights up.

"Oh yes! I thought you would never ask." Klank grabs the nearest oak tree, snaps it in half, and charges the towering T. rex, swinging the oak like a battle ax.

"My pleasure," beeps Klink, revving his ATV engine, rocking on his oversize camping tires, readying to sprint into action.

Klank rams the surprised T. rex with his tree trunk.

Frank and Janegoodall run out and scatter a sweet trail of energy bar bits, luring the ANT toward them.

"Boom!" yells Klank, smacking the T. rex on one side. **"Bam!"** he yells, spanking the T. rex on the other.

Klink zips out and snags the EvoBlaster Belt with his hook extension.

But unseen by anyone, the rushing water of the now-raging stream undercuts the sandy bank. It leaves no support for the tallest sycamore tree (*Platanus occidentalis*) . . . that falls with a splintering *CRAAAASHHHHH* . . . cutting Klink . . . and the Belt . . . off from Frank.

Klank pauses, looks over to help Klink.

And in that split second of inattention, the T. rex lunges at Klank and chomps the big robot's head completely off.

CHOMP

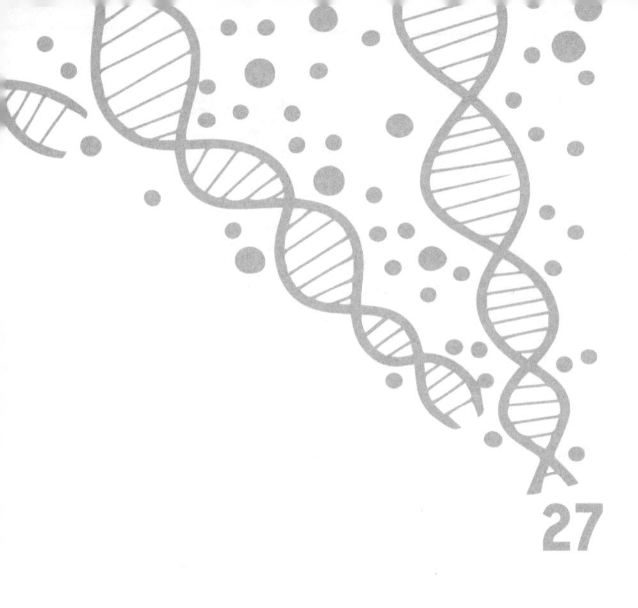

27

CALCULATING.

Analyzing.

Concluding.

Planning.

Klink performs all these thought processes in his robot brain as he surveys the scene of trapped humans, evolution mistakes, and his destroyed robot friend, Klank.

He instantly reviews his Three Laws of Robotics.

Law One: A robot cannot injure a human, or let a human be injured by not helping.

Law Two: A robot must obey orders from humans. Though not if those orders break Law One.

Law Three: A robot must protect its own life. As long as that does not break Law One or Law Two.

In less than a second, Klink arrives at the most rational plan.

"Throw me the belt!" Frank calls from behind the downed tree.

But then the T. rex stomps on Klank's headless body, smashing it into twisted metal bits.

Klink watches. And something white-hot mad floods his circuits.

"Hurry!" yells Frank.

The T. rex and jumbo ANT both turn their hungry eyes back on the *Homo sapiens*.

"Meowwwwww!" pleads *Felis catus watson*, above on the tree branch.

Klink's webcam eye turns blood-red. His internal engine revs to max. He leans back and blasts, louder than he has ever yelled, a sonic-boom loud:

"KLAAAAAAAANK!"

His entire robot body sparking, Klink rejects the rational plan.

Klink narrows his eye to laser-beam focus.

Klink deliberately straps the EvoBlaster Belt on himself.

Klink turns away from the *Homo sapiens,* and rolls toward the evo-monsters who have crushed his friend.

"Don't do it!" yells Frank. "Your circuits can't handle a triple-DNA evo-blast!"

Klink rolls forward. He knows exactly what his circuits can handle. And he doesn't care.

"BAWWWWKKKK!" roars the hungry T. rex.

"CHCHCHCHCH!" adds the whopper ANT.

They both advance on their human breakfast.

Janegoodall and Frank try their best to hide behind the fallen tree. Janegoodall marvels. "Amazing life forms . . . but they are getting a bit close for comfort now . . ."

"Meow meow meowwww!" warns *Felis catus watson* from up above.

Frank shakes his head. "If I could just get the belt . . ."

Klink rolls toward the T. rex and ANT. He rewires the **FAST-FORWARD** and **REVERSE** buttons. He connects one last attachment, not one hundred percent certain it will work.

"Oh no," says Janegoodall. "What is he doing? This is no time for roasting hot dogs."

Mr. Chimp has seen all he needs to see. He realizes he has no chance for anything good in this fight. He swings away through the treetops.

The colossal ANT snaps its killer jaws.

The T. rex gnashes its jagged teeth.

Klink charges at full speed. He points the rewired EvoBlaster Belt with Three-Pronged Hot Dog Roasting Fork at T. rex, ANT, and *Felis catus watson.*

The undammed Darwin stream water thunders. Blue jays (*Cyanotta cristata*) screech. Crickets (*Grillus campestris*) fiddle-screech.

Klink presses **EVO-PLAY**.

The EvoBlaster Belt compass spin-fires three wireless bolts of DNA-blasting energy out Klink's hot dog attachment.

Felis catus watson wavers.

The charging dinosaur and gargantuan ANT shimmer.

DNA strands unravel, reform, mutate, blur, evolve, devolve.

But it doesn't work.

There is not enough energy to power three evo-changes.

Klink stalls, grinds to a halt, and falls over.

The T. rex and jumbo ANT advance on Frank and Janegoodall.

Frank Einstein knows why the triple charge didn't work. Sadly, he also knows Klink will not survive the energy unravel. But now it's the only way. Frank calls to Klink. "You have to switch to **WELL-DONE**!"

Klink blinks. Of course.

He quickly flips the Three-Pronged Hot Dog Roasting Fork setting switch to **WELL-DONE** and punches **EVO-PLAY**.

Three new charges spit out of the three prongs.

With his metal heart power source and the molecular structure of all his metal parts feeding the three evo-blasts, Klink starts to disintegrate into atomic pieces.

Dinosaur, ANT, and *Felis catus watson* fuzz.

Klink, disappearing, still holds the **EVO-PLAY** button down hard.

And with one final triple-loud *BAM!,* Klink, the belt, the T. rex, the mammoth ANT, and *Felis catus watson* . . . disappear.

28

THE CLEARING IN THE MIDDLE OF DARWIN PARK IS ALMOST DEAD quiet. No bird songs, no animal calls, no insect noises.

The only sound is the soothing splash and gurgle of the restored Darwin River.

Frank Einstein and Janegoodall stand at the bank of the moving water.

Anna picks up a still-hungry baby chick.

"Peep peep peep."

Janegoodall holds a bug in the palm of her hand. "The mighty ant."

"Oh no," says Frank. "Where is . . . where is . . . ?" He can't bring himself to say his best friend's name.

"Hey!" yells Watson from a tree branch overhead. "How am I supposed to get down from here?"

"Watson! You're OK! We knew you could do it!"

Frank and Janegoodall help Watson get down from the tree.

Together they pick up the broken bits and pieces of Klank and put them in Janegoodall's backpack.

They look for anything left of Klink.

But all they find is a melted rubber handle of his Three-Pronged Hot Dog Roasting Fork.

29

UNBELIEVABLE!" SAYS GRAMPA AL, SMACKING THE STEERING WHEEL of his souped-up Fix It! shop truck. "It was that dippy T. Edison kid behind all this? Again? Dang. I should have known."

Frank nods.

"And so he was the one who hacked my top secret communicator? And sent me off on a wild goose chase?"

"Yes," says Janegoodall, riding in the back, carefully cradling her backpack full of Klank pieces. "He and Mr. Chimp were stealing water out of the Darwin River, selling it as Nature Good spring water from Fiji, and ruining the entire ecosystem."

Grampa Al steers the truck around a tricky curve.

"Just shows you—don't mess with nature. It's all connected. You wreck one piece, you mess up all kinds of things you don't know about."

Frank looks out the window, watches the forest whipping by. "Man, but that EvoBlaster is one really great invention."

Watson grabs Frank. "Don't ever mention that thing again! Ever! I mean it."

Frank nods, "OK, OK. And . . . Watson?"

Watson, thinking Frank is going to say something nice about how worried he was, how much he missed him, and how sorry he was for making an invention that almost got him stuck forever as a cat . . . asks, "What?"

Frank looks into Watson's eyes and says, *"Meow."*

Janegoodall laughs.

"RRRRARRRRRRRR!" Watson punches Frank in the arm.

Frank and Watson wrestle. Headlocks, arm bars, elbow jams, and noogies. Happy that everyone is safe, and that they are kings of the food chain once again.

"Uncle. Uncle!" says Frank. "You win."

Watson flexes both arms. "Ohhhh yeah."

Frank rubs his head. "But you have to admit the EvoBlaster Belt is a completely amazing invention."

"OK," says Watson. "It *was* pretty cool."

Frank adds. "But I would give it all up if it would bring back Klink."

Grampa Al looks in his rearview mirror at Janegoodall and her backpack.

"Little bit of work and fix-it care, I'm sure we can get Klank back together."

"Yeah . . ." Frank looks out the window again.

They probably can put Klank back together.

But the unspoken sentence is—there is no putting Klink back together.

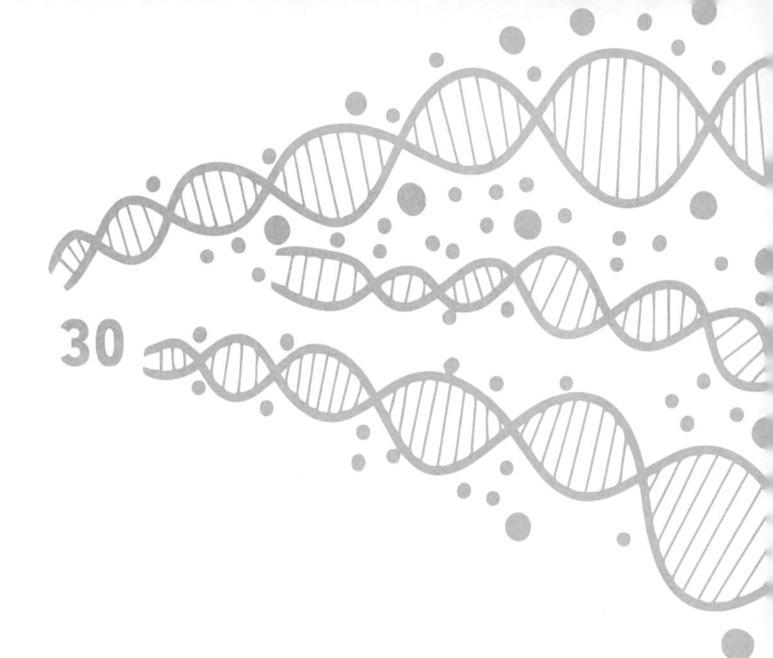

30

"UNBELIEVABLE!" SAYS T. EDISON, SMACKING THE WALNUT-AND-leather dashboard of the black Edison limousine. "That annoying, stupid Frank Einstein messes up my genius plan? Again? Idiot! I should have known."

Mr. Chimp nods.

He pulls his chauffeur cap low and drives carefully over the potholed dirt road out of Darwin Park, heading back to Midville.

He can't even begin to think about his crushing disappointment. How close he was. What he could have been. All he could have done if only—

"Watch where you are going!" shrieks T. Edison. "What are you doing?!"

Mr. Chimp steers smoothly around the hole in the road.

He takes one hand off the steering wheel, and truthfully signs:

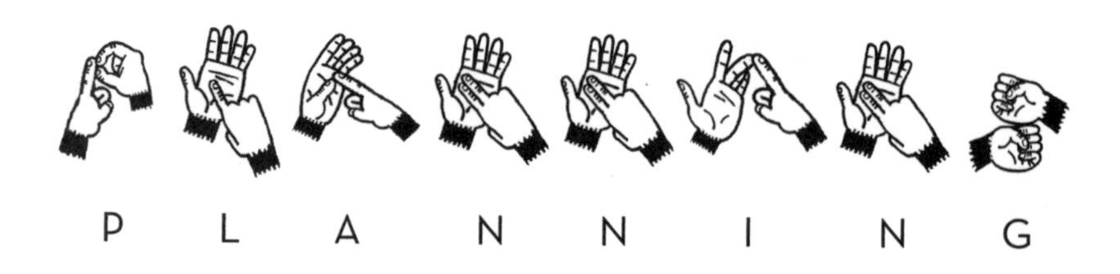

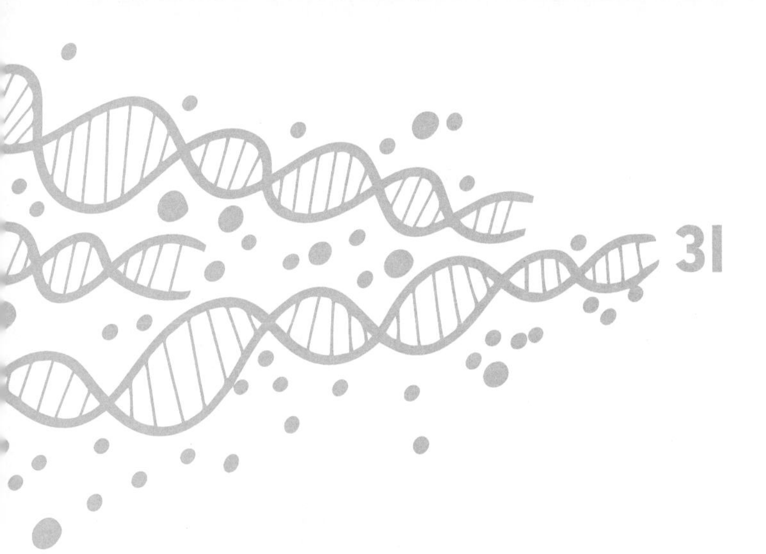

31

DUSK.

A great horned owl (*Bubo virginianus* . . . and yes—the exact same owl Frank and Watson heard, and Janegoodall and her Science Scout pals saw) pukes up a pellet.

It hits the ground with a wet plop.

Inside the pellet is a mouse jawbone, a bird rib, and a rat tooth.

There is also, recently hooked on the outside of the pellet, a small knot of wires, a mini memory chip, and a tiny battery.

Bent. Scorched. Woven together. Almost heart shaped.

The impact of the pellet hitting the ground triggers the beat-up remains to switch on.

The owl launches itself from its high wall perch, and, predator perfect, glides silently away into the gathering dark.

The small wire heart sends out a signal.

Ring-Ring . . .

Ring-Ring . . .

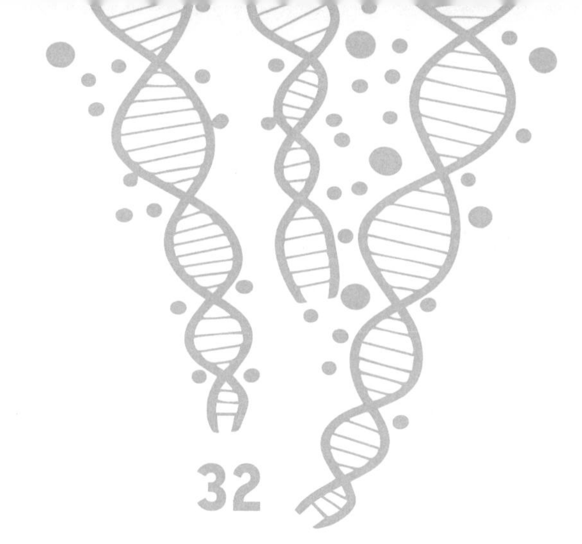

32

RING-RING . . .

Ring-Ring . . .

Grampa Al, Watson, Janegoodall, and Frank Einstein look at one another in surprise.

Frank reaches into Janegoodall's backpack, pulls out what's left of the ringing Klank phone, and answers it.

"Hello?"

"Latitude Forty One Point Two Two Six Nine One. Longitude Eight Six Point Four Three Nine Three Three Seven Three. Requesting pick-up."

"What?" says Frank.

"Latitude Forty One Point Two Two Six Nine One. Longitude Eight Six Point Four Three Nine

Three Three Seven Three," repeats the voice on the speakerphone.

It takes everyone a second. But Watson recognizes the voice first.

"Klink!"

"None other."

"How? What? Where?" asks Frank.

Grampa Al wheels the Fix It! shop truck around in a 180 dirt-cloud fishtail. "Klink's calling in his latitude and longitude." Grampa Al types the coordinates into his GPS and punches the accelerator. "I'm on it!"

"You didn't think I would let myself unravel with no plan for reassembly, did you?"

"No," says Frank. "But why couldn't we find you?"

"I got a bit sidetracked by a passing owl."

"Klink, we missed you!" says Watson.

"You are a hero," says Janegoodall. "You saved us. And you were soooooo mad!"

"I do not have emotions," says Klink. "So I could not have been mad."

Frank Einstein raises an eyebrow in disbelief.

"But you better come and get my core out of this filthy, disgusting owl regurgitation . . . BEFORE I GET WHITE-HOT, DNA-UNRAVELING CRAZY!"

"OK, OK," says Frank. "We are on our way. But let's also get started on our next mission."

"What?" asks Watson. "Fixing Klank?"

Frank pulls out his phone and displays a glowing screen. "Yes, but also the next column of our Wall of Science."

Frank Einstein swipes to show a blue-green circle.

"Oh boy," says Watson, not exactly one hundred percent enthusiastically.

Grampa Al stomps on the gas and flies down the dirt road at top speed.

"Planet Earth," says Watson nervously.

"And I already have a great idea," says Frank Einstein inventively. "Are you with me?"

"Absolutely," says Janegoodall.

"I am," says Klink.

Watson buckles his seat belt. "Do I have a choice?"

MATTER
Aristotle
E=mc2

ENERGY
newton
Tesla

HUMANS
daVinci

LIFE

EARTH

UNIVERSE

Darwin

FRANK EINSTEIN'S EVOBLASTER NOTEBOOK

"Imagination is more important than knowledge. For knowledge is limited, whereas imagination embraces the entire world, stimulating progress, giving birth to evolution."

—ALBERT EINSTEIN

"Evolution is the fundamental idea in all of Life Science."

—BILL NYE, *UNDENIABLE: EVOLUTION AND THE SCIENCE OF CREATION*

"No one is dumb who is curious. The people who don't ask questions remain clueless throughout their lives."

—NEIL DEGRASSE TYSON

"Heaven and earth and I are of the same root. The ten-thousand things and I are of one substance."

—SENG-CHAO, CHINESE BUDDHIST PHILOSOPHER, BORN 384 CE

"There is grandeur in this view of life, with its several powers, having been originally breathed into a few forms or into one; and that, whilst this planet has gone cycling on according to the fixed law of gravity, from so simple a beginning endless forms most beautiful and most wonderful have been, and are being, evolved."

—CHARLES DARWIN, LAST SENTENCE OF *ON THE ORIGIN OF SPECIES*

WATSON'S AMAZING INVENTIONS BASED ON THE LIVING WORLD

1. In 1948, a Swiss man named George de Mestral was out walking in the mountains with his dog. George was amazed at how strongly the burrs stuck to his dog's fur and to his own coat. He looked at the burrs under his microscope and saw that the burrs had hundreds of little hooks that snagged loops in fabric or fur.

He decided to imitate this design, with tiny hooks on one side and loops on the other, to make a fastener that was better than a zipper.

He combined the "vel" from "velvet" and "cro" from "crochet" to name his invention: VELCRO.

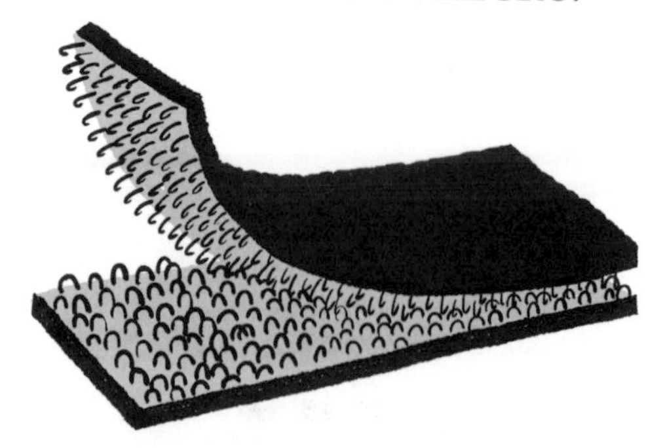

2. Fish, sharks, dolphins, and whales all use tails and flippers to push themselves through water.

In the early 1700s, a boy who lived near the water in Boston wanted to move faster through the water. So he made flipper-shaped sandals to attach to his feet.

This inventor is on the U.S. hundred dollar bill.

GRAMPA AL'S MILITARY CORNER

MILITARY TIME

To prevent mixing up times (such as 6:00 in the morning and 6:00 in the evening), the military uses a twenty-four-hour clock instead of a twelve-hour clock.

Beginning with midnight as 0000 hour, each hour is the next 100:

Midnight 12:00 = 0000 hours	Noon 12:00 = 1200 hours
1:00 AM = 0100 hours	1:00 PM = 1300 hours
2:00 AM = 0200 hours	2:00 PM = 1400 hours
3:00 AM = 0300 hours	3:00 PM = 1500 hours
4:00 AM = 0400 hours	4:00 PM = 1600 hours
5:00 AM = 0500 hours	5:00 PM = 1700 hours
6:00 AM = 0600 hours	6:00 PM = 1800 hours
7:00 AM = 0700 hours	7:00 PM = 1900 hours
8:00 AM = 0800 hours	8:00 PM = 2000 hours
9:00 AM = 0900 hours	9:00 PM = 2100 hours
10:00 AM = 1000 hours	10:00 PM = 2200 hours
11:00 AM = 1100 hours	11:00 PM = 2300 hours

MILITARY ALPHABET

To prevent mixing up letters that sound alike when spoken over a radio, important military communications use words to represent each letter of the alphabet.

A = Alpha
B = Bravo
C = Charlie
D = Delta
E = Echo
F = Foxtrot
G = Golf
H = Hotel
I = India
J = Juliet
K = Kilo
L = Lima
M = Mike
N = November
O = Oscar
P = Papa
Q = Quebec
R = Romeo
S = Sierra
T = Tango
U = Uniform
V = Victor
W = Whiskey
X = X-ray
Y = Yankee
Z = Zulu

So if you wanted to spell DARWIN, you would say: "**D**elta, **A**lpha, **R**omeo, **W**hiskey, **I**ndia, **N**ovember."

—GRAMPA ALPHA LIMA

KLINK AND KLANK PRESENT:
HOW TO MAKE YOUR OWN EVOBLASTER BELT

MATERIALS

1 World Championship wrestling belt

1 Magnetic compass

1 Circular diagram of all 1.9 million forms of connected life

2 TV Remotes (with >>, SELECT, << buttons)

1 High-speed DNA Double Helix Un-Zipper

1 High-speed DNA Double Helix Re-Zipper

1 Three-Pronged Hot Dog Roasting Fork

Wire, lights, switches, buttons, springs, buns, and mustard

ASSEMBLY

Remove gold center medallion of Championship belt.

Place circular life diagram in middle belt section.

Measure space in belt to insert DNA Un-Zipper directly in—

"Why are elephants wrinkled?"

"Klank, I am explaining how to build an EvoBlaster Belt. Do not interrupt."

Measure space in belt to insert—

"Did you ever try to iron one?"

"No. I am not going to think about this. You will not make my circuits blow. Again."

Measure space in belt to—

"What time is it when an elephant sits on your fence?"

"I do not know. I do not want to know."

"Time to get a new fence."

"Bzzzzt . . . bzzzz . . . NO! I. Will. Not. Think. About. Elephants."

Measure space in belt to—

"What did the peanut say to the elephant?"

"Bzzzzt . . . bzzzz . . . AIEEEEEEEEEE! What? WHAT? WHAT DID THE PEANUT SAY TO THE ELE-PHANT?!"

"Nothing. Peanuts cannot talk. Ha ha ha. Ha ha ha."

"Noooooooooooo POP! bzzzz
zzzzzzzzzzzzzzzzzzzzzzzz
zzzzzzzzzzzzzzzzzzzzzzzzz
zzzzzzzzzzzzzzzzzzzzzzzzzz
zzzzzzzzzzzzzzzzzzzzzzzzzzzz
zzzzzzzzzzzzzzzzzzzzzzzzzzzzzzzzzzzzzzzzzzzzzz

SCIENCE SCOUT LEADER MS. PRISCILLA'S LIVING THING HALL OF FAME

BIGGEST

- The heaviest insect is probably a Goliath beetle (*Golianthus regius*): 100 grams.
- The largest reptile is the saltwater crocodile (*Crocodylus porosus*): 1,360 kilograms.
- The heaviest bird is the ostrich (*Struthio camelus*): 156 kilograms, with a 1.4 kilogram egg.

- The biggest animal to ever exist on Earth is the Blue Whale (*Balaenoptera musculus*): 100 feet (thirty meters), weighing up to 200 tons.

- But the biggest living thing on Earth is either: a group of quaking aspen trees (*Populus tremuloides*) in Utah: 47,000 trees, genetically identical, connected below ground, weighing 6,000 tons (or about forty Blue Whales);

or, a spread of honey mushrooms (*Armillaria ostoyae*) in Oregon: genetically identical, connected below ground, covering 2,385 acres (the equivalent of 1,700 football fields or four square miles). Could also be between 2,400 and 8,650 years old.

FASTEST

- A sailfish (*Istiophorus albicans*) can swim 68 miles (109 kilometers) per hour.
- Cheetahs (*Acinonyx jubatus*) can run 75 miles (120 kilometers) per hour.
- The Peregrine Falcon (*Falco peregrinus*) can reach a maximum airspeed of 242 miles (389 kilometers) per hour.
- But the organism that travels the fastest by far are the spores of the "Hat Thrower," or dung cannon fungus (*Pilobolus crystallinus*).

The spores look like little black hats.

And this fungus grows on animal dung (i.e.: poop).

This fungus shoots its spores at 20,000 G-Forces.

A trained jet fighter pilot can withstand maybe nine Gs.

Most people pass out at four Gs.

STRONGEST

- The eagle (*Haliaeetus leucocephalus*) is the strongest bird. Able to lift four times its own weight.
- The anaconda snake (*Eunectes murinus*) can squeeze something that weighs its same 250 kilogram weight to death.
- The African elephant (*Loxodonta africana*) is the strongest land animal. Able to carry 9,000 kilograms (or the equivalent of 130 men).
- The leafcutter ant (*Atta cephalote*) can lift and carry an object fifty times its body weight. That would be like you lifting and carrying a car with your teeth.
- But the strongest animal on Earth, able to pull 1,140 times its own weight (which would be like you pulling six busses full of people), is the Dung beetle (*Orthophagus taurus*).

WEIRDEST

- The Vampire Flying Frog (*acophorus vampyrus*)

Lives in the mountain jungles of Vietnam. Can glide up to fifty feet using the webbing between their toes. Called vampires because, as tadpoles, they have curved black fangs sticking out of the undersides of their mouths.

- Mind-Control Fungus (*Opiocordyceps unilateralis*)

Infects ants, takes over their brains, then kills the zombie ant once it moves to a good location . . . for spreading spores, and growing more fungus.

• Bristle Worms (Polychaeta)

Terrifying-looking sea worms, they live miles undersea, near hydrothermal vents on the ocean floor.

Though luckily, most are a little more than three inches in length.

MR. CHIMP'S FAMILY TREE

HOMO SAPIENS

PAN TROGLODYTES

GORILLA GORILLA

MR. CHIMP'S
ALPHABET
A
B
C
D
E
F
G
H
I
J
K
L
M
N
O
P
Q
R
S
T
U
V
W
X
Y
Z

MATTER
ENERGY
HUMANS

LIFE

EARTH

UNIVERSE

JON SCIESZKA is thrilled with the recent discovery that living humans all have a bit of Neanderthal in them. Though he is also happy he evolved to become the author of a lot of books, the founder of Guys Read, and the first National Ambassador for Young People's Literature. He makes his hominid nest in Brooklyn, New York.

BRIAN BIGGS has illustrated books by Garth Nix, Cynthia Rylant, and Katherine Applegate, and is the writer and illustrator of the Everything Goes series, as well as the brand-new series for Abrams Appleseed, Tinyville Town. He lives in Philadelphia, Pennsylvania.

TO OUR CLOSEST LIVING PRIMATE RELATIVES—
CHIMPANZEES AND BONOBOS

LIBRARY OF CONGRESS CATALOGING-IN-PUBLICATION DATA HAS BEEN APPLIED FOR AND MAY BE OBTAINED FROM THE LIBRARY OF CONGRESS.

ISBN: 978-1-4197-2379-7

BOOK DESIGN BY CHAD W. BECKERMAN

PRINTED AND BOUND IN U.S.A.
10 9 8 7 6 5 4 3 2 1

ABRAMS The Art of Books
161-165 Farringdon Road
London, UK EC1R 3AL
www.abramsandchronicle.co.uk

ALSO AVAILABLE:

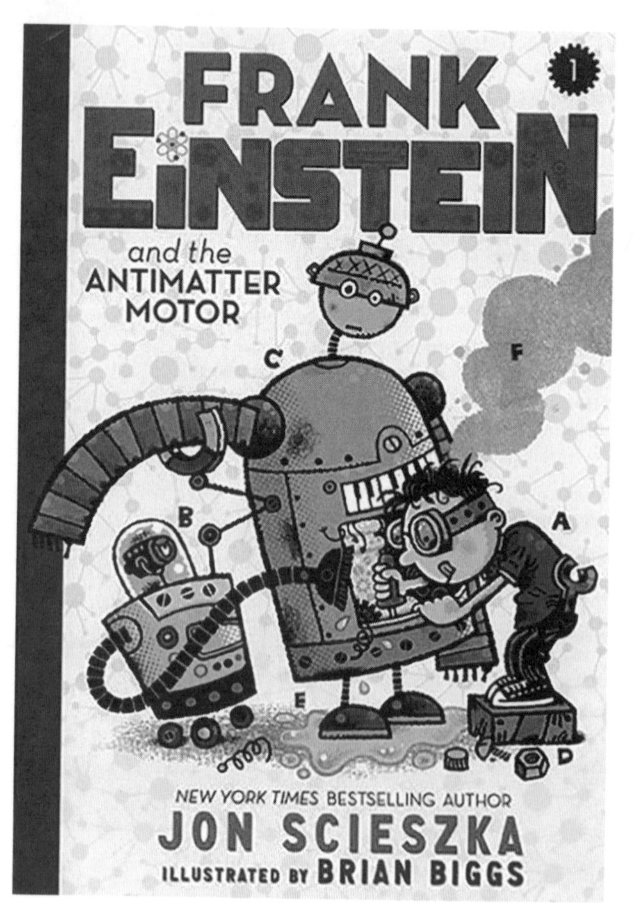

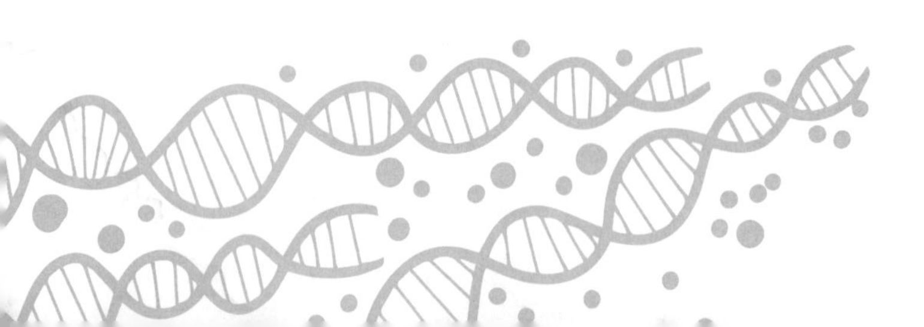

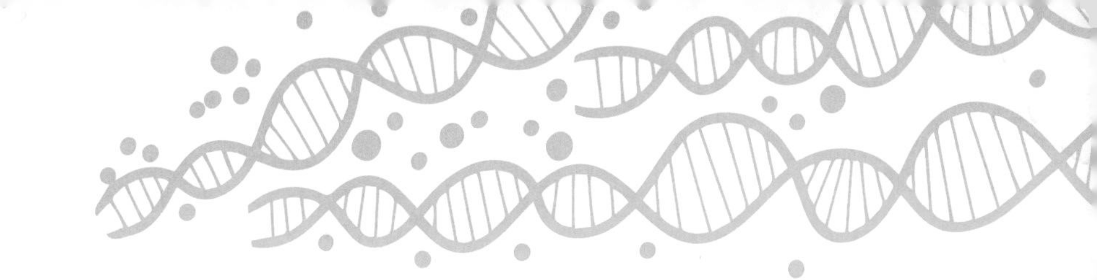

NK
TEIN
2
ESTSELLING AUTHOR
IESZKA
RIAN BIGGS

3
FRANK
EINSTEIN
and the
BRAINTURBO
THE NEW YORK TIMES BESTSELLING SERIES
JON SCIESZKA
ILLUSTRATED BY BRIAN BIGGS

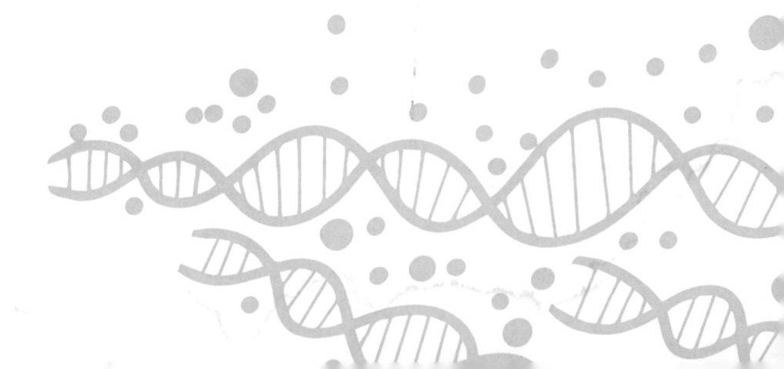

COMING SPRING 2017